A Brush with Death

Brandon and the others watched as Jere Sublette, with four guns held inches from his head, was unwrapped from his cocoon of rope and thrust inside the wooden cube of a jail—which was constructed of heavy timbers—and locked in behind its massive door.

"I got a spare buggy top," liveryman Ed Marks said. "Bring yours in and I'll replace the one that crazy bastard shot away. Sublette really had it in for you, didn't he?" Marks grimaced. "There ain't nothing scarier than a crazy man. And if it's a crazy man with a gun, it's the worst it can get. You come out of it lucky, Mr. Blake."

Elise and the rest came up against a crazy man with a gun, Brandon thought, and they weren't lucky. Was Sublette one of Gren's gang? The farmer stuff doesn't fit, but a lot of the rest does. And if I did find out it was him, what then? Marks is right, he's crazy—madhouse crazy. No court would let him stand trial, no jurisdiction would execute him, not that I give a damn about that.

But if he's insane, can *I* execute him?

Also by D. R. Bensen

Rawhide Moon (Tracker #5)
The Renegade (Tracker #4)
Death in the Hills (Tracker #3)
Fool's Gold (Tracker #2)
Mask of the Tracker (Tracker #1)

Published by POCKET BOOKS

THE TRACKER #6

→ Deathwind ←

D.R. BENSEN

POCKET BOOKS

New York   London   Toronto   Sydney   Tokyo   Singapore

This book is a work of fiction. Names, characters, places, and
incidents are either products of the author's imagination or are used
fictitiously. Any resemblance to actual events or locales or persons,
living or dead, is entirely coincidental.

An *Original* Publication of POCKET BOOKS

POCKET BOOKS, a division of Simon & Schuster Inc.
1230 Avenue of the Americas, New York, NY 10020

ISBN: 0-671-73839-9

First Pocket Books printing June 1993

10 9 8 7 6 5 4 3 2 1

POCKET and colophon are registered trademarks of
Simon & Schuster Inc.

Cover art by Bill Dodge

Printed in the U.S.A.

→ Deathwind ←

1

Above a field of sunflowers that stood higher than an army of men turning their bland faces to the sun, a windmill rose on spindly legs like a single giant flower itself, with its wooden petals spread to catch the wind. Cole Brandon could see more of them across the farmlands, one a quarter mile away, others more distant, their positions shifting as the train drew him past them.

The Nonpareil Company's leaflet, open for study on his lap, was positively lyrical about them.

> These marvels of the inventor's genius and the mechanic's art may be harnessed to do many kinds of useful work; e.g., ginning cotton, sawing wood, shucking corn, and grinding feed. But it is as pumps, powered by the providential powers of the winds of air, that they achieve their true triumph, making possible a reliable supply of water to the farms that have civilized the western expanses of our Nation during the first century of its Independence.

That was a bit of commercial license, Brandon thought, since neither the windmills nor the farms in the "western expanses" had been there until the last twenty years or so. During most of the hundred years since 1776 the farmlands he was passing now, and those out toward Nebraska and beyond, had been open prairie or forest, the home of Indians, buffalo, and an arkload of creatures. Even a couple of years back, if he remembered right, there had been more open land along the railroad line and fewer farms. The West was filling up so fast that in a while it might look as if it had been settled for a hundred years, so the Nonpareil writer might not be too far off, just anticipating a little, as he had done with the exhortation to visit the company's exhibit in the Machinery Hall at the Centennial Exposition in Philadelphia. The last newspaper account Brandon had seen said that it looked after all as if the Exposition would open on time a month from now, so those eager to see Nonpareil's latest products would have at least that long a wait.

Brandon wondered if the exhibit would promote sales. Nonpareil certainly hoped so, as did the legion of other exhibitors and, in fact, most of the country. Many of the news stories about the Exposition had been candid about its hoped-for effect—to prime the pump of economy that had been gathering rust since the stock market panic almost three years ago. Celebrating a past that—however full of gore and glory it was—had been in many ways dismal and uncivilized was not what the Centennial Exposition was about; it was about demonstrating the wonders of the present age and the near future.

Brandon had for the last two and a half years taken about as little interest in politics and business as was possible for anyone more concerned than a prairie dog to do, but he had still seen the impact of the depression all through the West and had sensed a growing awareness that it was time for a change, and that some way or another it would happen. Whoever got elected in November, the tired, stained, shabby Grant administration would be out, and someone else would be in. Maybe no better, but at least new, and that would be something.

Not the best time to go into business selling windmills,

Brandon thought. The farmers need them, but they'll have a hard time scraping up enough to pay for them.

He smiled thinly. That would be worrisome if he gave a quarter of a damn if he ever sold a single windmill.

Brandon added up the penciled jots that registered the numbers of different kinds of windmills he had seen from the train window so far. Four that had the distinctive "boat tail" rear vanes of the Nonpareil, but many more Eclipses and a few of the hinge-vaned Halladay types, as best he could make out from studying the engravings that adorned the firms' leaflets. Nonpareil seemed to be doing the worst of the bunch; that would be the one to go to, then. A hungry business doesn't ask too many questions. Nonpareil was in Chicago, so he would have a train change in Kansas City, up to Des Moines, then across. Straight to St. Louis and up would be more convenient, but St. Louis was as closed to Cole Brandon as Mecca or the Chinese emperor's Forbidden City in Peking.

There had been no windmills to add to the survey for some time. The train had left the belt of farms and was passing through an area of woods and low bluffs, some of which edged the railroad line as though it were a river flowing through steep banks. An angry scream of the whistle came from the locomotive ahead, and the car bucked suddenly, slowed and jolted to a stop, throwing the passengers forward. Brandon's head slammed against the back of the seat in front of him, and the windmill companies' leaflets cascaded onto the floor.

He cursed and bent to pick them up. As he scrabbled them together he heard a chorus of passenger comment: "Cow on the tracks," "Flat wheel," "Mebbe run over a hobo," "Naw, wouldn't make that much of a jolt, a couple tons of loco runs over a man, it's like a cleaver through a mouse," "Oh, Jesus!"

Brandon was suddenly sure that the last speaker was not commenting on the vivid metaphor, particularly as his words were followed by absolute silence.

Brandon eased his head around the side of the seat. Two seats ahead of him, about the same distance from the front of the car, he saw a stocky man in dusty breeches and boots and a long jacket, face masked by a bandanna tucked under his hat. The mask was presumably thin enough to see through, for he traversed the muzzle of the heavy revolver he held to cover the passengers with a persuasive air of confidence. Another man similarly dressed and holding a canvas sack stood in the doorway to the vestibule.

"Ease out the valybles, wallets an' watches, pokes an' pretties, ladies an' gents," the first man said. "We keep it calm an' easy, an' we go away the richer an' you get to keep breathin', so's we all of us benefit by the experience."

Brandon, still crouched, eased his head back behind the seat. He could not see the train robber now but could place him accurately as he moved down the aisle one slow step at a time.

"We ain't the James boys, folks—" No, you're not, Brandon thought; whatever the Jameses are, it isn't half-witted. "—just working men with no work in this cruel depression, gettin' by as best we can. So if you'll have your money, jewels, and what-all out as I pass by, my partner'll see to the collection, and it'll all be done with before you can say son of a *bitch* oh shit damn!"

As the train robber came abreast of him Brandon drove at him, one hand clamping over the man's gun hand, the other gripping him by the loose crotch of his trousers and what it covered, then rose out of his crouch, pivoting, pointing the robber at the window, and letting go. The whole sequence of motions seemed almost effortless to Brandon, and in a way unintended; he had formed no plan when he saw the robbers enter the car and had done what he had done as instinctively as a wolf leaps for the throat of its prey.

The screaming bandit's head shattered the glass, and his flailing feet vanished through the suddenly vacant window frame. A sharper noise than a thump cut his wail short; it sounded to Brandon as if he had hit a rock or a tie, something harder than grassy earth. He found that he was holding the man's revolver, and that it was pointing in the general direction of the sack-holder, who stared at him in shocked disbelief and seemed to be reaching with preternatural slowness for the holstered gun at his side.

Brandon ignored the shouts and screams from the passengers and twice squeezed the trigger of the revolver he held. It was a self-cocking double-action model, like his own .38, tidily but uselessly packed in his valise, and it fired with each trigger pull.

The robber vanished backwards into the vestibule, dropping his sack. Brandon doubted he had hit him and ran to the vestibule. He saw the bandit start to scramble down the car steps, catch his boot toe on a projection, and fall heavily to the rocky ground, face first. His companion lay a few feet away, unmoving.

Brandon jumped from the vestibule, clearing the steps, and landed on the prone robber's torso; he felt a crunching and yielding under his boots and heard a shrill, bubbling scream. Some ribs stove in, if nothing worse.

He spun and looked toward the head of the train. As he expected, he saw a man standing on a low bluff, holding a shotgun pointed squarely at the locomotive's cab. It was curious that though he could see the smallest details with absolute clarity, the colors of what he saw were muted, or rather filmed, as if he were viewing a photograph that had been tinted with a wash of red. He could also see, beyond the massive driving wheels and boiler, the edge of the cowcatcher and the heavy log that protruded over the track, a simple but effective way of stopping the train, as one man could guard the engineer and fireman and the other two could relieve the passengers of their possessions in safety and convenience. That was the plan, anyhow.

Again without conscious thought he triggered off two shots at the shotgun holder, saw the gun fly into the air and turn over once before hitting the ground as its owner bent over like a man who starts a back somersault but then abandons the idea in favor of lying on the ground, twisting like a beheaded snake, and yelling loudly.

Brandon could feel the drying rush of air on his teeth and in his mouth as he breathed shallowly and rapidly, darting a glance at each of the would-be train robbers in turn. His first victim was quite still, the second was whimpering liquidly at his feet, and the third was calling for someone to keep him from bleeding to death. No danger from them, then, and no need to put another bullet in any of them, Brandon concluded with a mild feeling of regret.

A babble of voices and other sounds—the hissing escape of steam from the stopped engine's boiler, the scrawks, chirps, and trills of birds in the low trees and tall grasses—flooded in on him, as did the actual colors of the scene and people around him. It was like waking up, and he had the feeling of having come out of some nightmare of fury and blood. The revolver felt like a twenty-pound weight in his hand, and the rage that had inflated and driven him drained away.

"My God, I never seed anything like that," one of the crowd of passengers who were now inspecting the battle-field and its casualties said. "Those fellows look like as if they'd come up against a band of Apaches, except they still got their skin on and their privates in place."

Brandon ignored the speaker, turned, and climbed the steps into the car.

"Given how he grabbed the one that went out the winder, I don't know if his are still on, or if they'll do him any good if they are," another passenger said after a quick glance showed him no women in immediate earshot.

Brandon entered the car, and the clatter and hum of comment from those passengers still in their seats stopped abruptly. He found his seat, laid the bandit's revolver on it, and bent down to pick up the windmill companies' leaflets.

A round face topped by a battered hat looked down, wide-eyed, over the back of the seat in front of him.

"That was some kind of swift," the face said to Brandon. "Like a twister goin' through a town and leavin' nought behind but matchsticks and the wailin' of the bereaved. But"—the face clouded with a touch of unease—"I dunno, weren't it a touch extreme? Wouldn't mean to criticize or offend, no, sir, but"—he glanced at the gun lying on the seat—"but it weren't like they was Injuns on a raid or some such, you know? They was just train robbers."

Brandon slid the leaflets together in a neat bundle, straightened up, took his seat again, then looked for the first time at the face perched on the seat back and said in flat tones, "I don't like train robbers."

2

The train jerked into motion, then picked up speed, and the landscape began to unreel past Brandon's window. He had taken another seat, and a trainman had tacked a square of boards over the punched-out window next to his previous seat to keep out the cinders that would otherwise have rained into the car. Brandon had handed over the bandit's revolver to the conductor and, without anything definite having been said, had come to an understanding that the conductor would get to pass on to the authorities the official account of the proceedings, amplifying his part in them as he might choose, and Brandon would be left out of it, spared both glory and questions.

What had happened had happened so fast that even those who had seen it might find themselves unsure of their eyes and memories, and in any case a heroic conductor would make a better story than an undistinguished and unknown, if unexpectedly lethal, passenger. He was aware of the glances thrown at him by the other occupants of the car and of the buzz of talk about him, and also aware that it was diminishing as their interest faded. There is only so much you can find to say about the back of a man's head, which, it was clear, was all they were going to see of him.

Brandon looked down at the leaflets and decided that he was disinclined to instruct himself further in the details of windmill construction and the virtues of the Eclipse over the Nonpareil or the Nonpareil over the Halladay. He supposed he would have no difficulty in explaining persuasively why the Nonpareil had no equal and the Halladay and Eclipse were junk, if in fact he wound up selling the Nonpareils; the practice of trial law was a wonderful training in finding, or confecting, arguments to prove any point whatever.

He looked out the window at the fields approaching, then receding past him. "I don't like train robbers." That was an understatement so extravagant as to be comic, except that there was nothing comic in the whole bloody business.

Given the rich vein of criminality in America, it was remarkable that regular railroad service had been in existence for almost half a century, transporting money-carrying passengers and shipments of currency, valuables, and gold, before it had occurred to anyone to rob a train. And given the near-total devotion to crime in all its forms of Peter and Quint Kenneally of Arkansas and their descendants unto the third generation, it was almost as remarkable that the innovator was not one of the clan. But Gren Kenneally, said to have been expelled from Quantrill's murderous guerrillas for excessive brutality, was quick to follow once the way had been shown.

On a fall day he and ten or so followers had stopped a Chicago, Rock Island & Pacific train north of St. Louis and robbed it, leaving the engineer, fireman, and clerks in the express car dead. Miles away they were recognized and closely pursued, and they took refuge in the main house of an isolated farm—Mound Farm, the property of St. Louis attorney Cole Brandon and his wife, Elise. On that day Elise Ostermann Brandon, her father, August Ostermann, and her aunt Gertrud were at Mound Farm for a relaxing visit; Cole Brandon stayed in the city to attend the retirement party of a judge he did not especially like.

By the time the pursuers came up, Mound Farm was in the hands of the Kenneally gang, and Elise, her father and aunt, and the farm's staff were hostages. There was an uneasy standoff until after nightfall, when Brandon, summoned from St. Louis, arrived in time to see their bodies carried out of the smoldering ruins of the buildings the robbers had fired to cover their escape into the darkness.

I don't like train robbers. . . .

Gren Kenneally and his men had a victim to their credit they did not know about. The Cole Brandon who had lived up to that day was in effect as dead as his wife. He worked mechanically, lived mechanically, and felt nothing. Even the chance of renewed life and feeling Elise's sister Krista offered when she admitted the emotions she had held for him over the years (and which Brandon had made an effort not to return during his marriage) was meaningless to him.

Two encounters renewed his energy and interest. One was with the bizarre mountain man Ned Norland, seasoned and hardened by half a century of trapping, hunting, fighting, scouting, trading, and, when possible, wenching. Norland's anarchic vitality and determinedly outrageous conduct stirred Brandon to amusement for the first time since Elise's murder, the first crack in the block of ice around him.

The other meeting, at night and at the now-deserted Mound Farm, left one of those who rode with Gren Kenneally dead, then buried in the Indian mound that gave the farm its name. And it marked the end of the long dying of Cole Brandon, Esq., of Walsh's Row, partner in Lunsford Ahrens & Brandon and sorrowing relict of Elise Ostermann Brandon, late of Walsh's Row but now a resident of Bellefontaine Cemetery. Standing in the smoke-blackened kitchen of Mound Farm with his hands stained with the robber's grave-dirt, Cole Brandon accepted his destiny.

He had killed one of them, and he was going to kill the others. Grief and rage did not seem to come into it, just a cold certainty. Cole Brandon was not a tracker of men, a killer, but Cole Brandon was only a shell covering a newly born creature that was nothing else.

He learned from Ned Norland to be patient and subtle in his tracking, to trust to intuition or even chance, and to assume any identity that would let him prowl the hunting ground but not be seen as a hunter. In the many, many months since that moment he had been half a dozen men under half a dozen names: a cattle buyer, a gambler, a wandering hardcase, a newspaper reporter, a temporary law officer, a trail cook. Of those who had helped Gren Kenneally rob and kill, six were dead now. Brandon had killed three, and the others had brought on their deaths because of what they were, but the main thing was that they were dead. Each death went into the scales to bring things nearer to a bearable balance.

Five left, and one of the five was Gren Kenneally, a man savage beyond even the scope of the Kenneallys. Brandon had been astonished when the list bearing the names or aliases of Gren Kenneally's confederates and the little that was known of them was handed to him by a respected small-town judge. The man explained that time and success had changed, or rather diversified, the Kenneallys. One group was still the notorious outlaw family with a hand in every type of crime, feared across a wide area of the country. But when crime does pay, something has to be done with the money, and Kenneallys and Kenneally kin had gone into business, finance, even politics, usually under new names. By now there was a second generation of them, often with hardly any ties to the original family—though when a crime-practicing Kenneally was caught, help could come from unexpected places, and when a Kenneally businessman had an inconvenient rival or labor unrest, such problems were often sorted out mysteriously but violently.

Gren was a monster, the judge said, and his outrages were bad for business; the massacre at Mound Farm was by no means the worst of what he had done. If a factory owner or politician were found to have ties to an old, established criminal clan, that could be glossed over, even seen as colorful; but any connection with Gren Kenneally would be utterly damning.

The consensus of those who spoke for both branches of the Kenneallys was that Cole Brandon, under whatever name or occupation he might be following, should have every help in tracking and killing Gren Kenneally and was welcome to any of the others he killed along the way. Gren and his men had scattered after Mound Farm, and little had been seen of them since. Brandon had picked up Gren Kenneally's trail in San Francisco, where Kenneally had won the enmity of a powerful tong leader who also gave Brandon his blessing—and, in later months, some long-range indirect assistance. But Kenneally had left San Francisco weeks before Brandon's arrival, and there had been no sight of him since.

"Like for dinner, sir?"

Brandon surfaced from his immersion in the past and looked up at the conductor. "Dinner?"

"Choice of five from the card here." He peeled an oblong of pasteboard from a sheaf he held and handed it to Brandon. "Steak, chicken, trout, ham, pork chops, each with vegetable platter and fried or boiled potato; also, today only, antelope steak; coffee with the meal and pie or cake after. Lemme know and I'll wire ahead, and it'll be ready and on the table when we stop."

Brandon looked at the bill of fare, headed in ornate type MARVEL HALLS.

"Wonderful things, these places," the conductor said. "Clean, good food served so's the passenger can eat and be back on the train in a quarter hour, a marvel of the age indeed. You'll have?"

"Not hungry," Brandon said. "I'll wait till Kansas City."

The conductor bent closer. "About that, when we get to K.C.? You won't be changing your mind and deciding to talk to the newspapers and such on your own? Not that you ain't got a right to, but I wouldn't want to say things that'd make me look foolish later."

"Credit's all yours," Brandon said. "I don't need gratitude from the railroad, and you could use it." *And I especially don't need a fine-detailed steel engraving of my phiz adorning the news sheets as a nemesis of train robbers. That'd be like putting on a wolf skin to go hunting sheep.*

"Fine," the conductor said. "I tell you, you keep the card, and if you decide you want a dinner, lemme know. There's still about twenty minutes before we have to have them wired in." He moved past Brandon and began soliciting the next passenger's dinner order.

Brandon tapped the word MARVEL on the card with his forefinger. Jess Marvell had picked the right name for her trackside eating houses, which were springing up all across the West, providing good food served quickly by the neat, white-aproned, green-clad corps of Marvel Girls, instead of the grease-and-gristle meals slopped out by slatterns that were the standard frontier fare.

There's a tangle for you, Counselor, he told himself. *Bright young hotel manager needs money for a plan, offers to gather information for a mysterious stranger; said stranger agrees he'll pay for whatever she can find out about the movements of men said to be involved in train robbery. She uses the money to start up a business that looks like it'll last; stranger uses information to go around the country and kill people.*

The information Jess Marvell and her even younger partner Rush Dailey had sent to Brandon under various aliases at post offices throughout the West had rarely provided useful leads; for their safety, he had not brought up the name of Kenneally when specifying what he wanted to know, since undue interest in Kenneally matters tended to be as fatal as consumption, only quicker. He valued it, though, for the contact with Jess Marvell it represented.

Twice in the last several months his and Jess Marvell's

paths had crossed, and each time, without anything being said, it became clear to Brandon that there was something important and powerful between them. If there was ever an end to his mission, and he survived that end, he would have to deal with whatever that was. Just as he would have to deal with the love and the future that Krista had plainly offered.

Jess Marvell's face was as clear in his mind as if it were reflected next to his own in the window. He could, with some effort, summon the memory of Krista as he had last seen her, bright in a shaft of spring sunlight in the study of his brick house on Walsh's Row.

Elise's face hovered indistinctly at the edge of memory, fading to be replaced by the sharper image of the polished granite with her name on it in Bellefontaine.

He put the Marvel Hall card aside and picked up the Nonpareil leaflet. The Kenneally list had given a hint that one man he sought might be involved in farming in Nebraska, and who could better travel throughout that area unsuspected of hidden motives than a man offering access to the farmer's greatest need, water?

The Nonpareil Wind Engine Company of Chicago—general manager, Ralph Catesby, according to the leaflet—needed a new salesman, though they might not know that until Brandon paid them a visit the day after tomorrow. Not as Cole Brandon, though. That name belonged to the man remembered with increasing dimness in St. Louis who had vanished long ago, and it would be worn again only when the mission was done and that man returned to existence—if he ever could.

A new name meant another chance to forget it at a bad moment, and he decided to re-employ one of those he had already gone by. Calvin Blake was the one that came most readily to mind, maybe because he had seen it in print most often, signed to stories in the Spargill, Colorado, *Chronicle* in his incarnation as a newspaperman.

The decision taken, Calvin Blake turned out to be hungrier than Cole Brandon had been a few moments before, and he turned to the Marvel Hall menu, marking the trout dinner with boiled potato, pie rather than cake, and signing the card with a firm *C. Blake*.

"You're asking me to put up a bond, then," Brandon said.

Ralph Catesby shook his head. "It serves as a surety, certainly, but it is actually an investment, Mr. Blake, an investment in the future of this great nation, and an investment that can scarcely fail to be repaid in full measure, pressed down and running over."

"It's an investment not too many people are eager to make, I'd say," Brandon observed, "or you wouldn't be making it a condition of being a traveler for your windmills."

"Well, if you do a good job of selling them, you'll be helping your investment, so it's an incentive," Catesby said. He was a stocky man of about forty with a harassed expression on his seamed face. He had told Brandon that he had started Nonpareil on the strength of his patent for a new and improved design of vane for windmills, claimed to make the wheel mechanism more reliably responsive to changes in the wind, and Brandon suspected that he was finding matters of business to be more troublesome than the complexities of invention.

Catesby confirmed this with his next statement. "One reason we can use the money right now is that a couple of agents we sent out in the usual way pocketed the payments on orders they took, then vanished, and I felt I had to make good on the orders, so there's a good number of Nonpareils out there pumping up water with not a penny to show for it here. And I figure, knowing as little as I do about business stuff, anybody smart enough to sell my windmills is smart enough to figure out a way to cheat me, no matter what precautions I take about ordering. So I figure if I've got a good chunk of a man's money as hostage, he'll deal square with me so's he can come back and get it later on."

The location of Nonpareil's office—a room on the second floor of a building that had to date from after the

Fire four and a half years ago but already looked decades old, on the borderline between the business district and a major saloon-and-brothel quarter—had suggested to Brandon that the firm was not prospering, and Catesby's business methods suggested that it was not likely to. As he had reminded himself on the train, so much the better for his purposes. A go-ahead, successful company might be inclined to want to know more about a salesman's background than that he had a thousand dollars to pledge.

"Original way of recruiting help," Brandon said. "Working well?"

"You'll be the first to take it up, Blake," Ralph Catesby said. "If you do."

"Well, I think I will," Brandon said. "You accredit me as a bona fide representative of Nonpareil, give me a pad of order forms and all the foofaraw about the windmills, and I'll invest the thousand and trust you to keep it fed and watered while I'm on the road. I'll have it here tomorrow."

Catesby peered at him, slight unease mixing with his pleasure. "Good," he said after a moment. "But now I'm wondering if there's something I'm overlooking with you, just like I did with those other fellows. I just hope you don't have some swindle planned that I haven't figured out."

"Nothing like that," Brandon said, reasonably truthfully. Hunting and killing a man isn't a swindle, after all.

"Ah, well, even if you do, I'll learn from it, and that'll be a mistake I won't have to make again," Catesby said. "There's always a bright side."

3

In the aftermath of his wife's death Cole Brandon had
planned to travel, possibly to Europe and possibly returning someday. He had made arrangements to transfer
most of his liquid assets to a Chicago bank, with the idea
of drawing on them, if he needed to, without arousing the
concern of friends and acquaintances, who would be sure
to pick up word of any transactions of his in a local bank.
He had asked Krista Ostermann to forward the income
from his inherited share in Elise's family's business to
Chicago.

Brandon left the arrangements in place when he
changed his plans and took up the quest for Gren
Kenneally and his men, letting the foreign travel story
stand. As it happened, he had not needed to draw on the
Chicago funds so far; he had started out with a substantial sum in cash and had had few heavy expenses, and
most of the identities he assumed involved jobs that paid
at least an adequate wage.

But a thousand dollars was well beyond his immediate
resources, and the morning after his interview with
Ralph Catesby he made his way to the Mercantile &

Industrial Bank on Washington and Dearborn. Brandon had in years past been to Chicago enough to be moderately familiar with the business district but now found himself completely disoriented. He had of course read extensive accounts of the Fire and the total destruction it had wrought, but some part of his mind preserved Chicago as he had known it, and this city might as well have been an enlarged version of one of the towns that had sprung from the prairie in the last five or ten years. He had no landmarks to navigate by, but at least the street names were the same, and when he got to it, the fortresslike facade of the M & I seemed to be a near reproduction of the original.

The emergency attentions of his hotel's laundry and barber had brought Brandon's clothing and general appearance up to bank-customer standards, and the clerk at the counter accepted his identification and paid out the cash without question.

After pushing the fat envelope under the grille to Brandon the clerk said, "Um, Brandon . . . what was . . . Would you wait a minute, sir?"

Brandon nodded and considered walking briskly out of the bank as soon as the clerk trotted away to the row of offices behind the counter. But the situation didn't have the feel of danger—say, of the Missouri law having discovered a body at Mound Farm and being anxious to question the owner of the property—and he forced himself to wait.

The clerk returned with a large envelope. "A letter came for you, care of the bank, and the manager asked us clerks to notice if you came in. A few months back it was, so's I nearly didn't remember."

Brandon took the envelope with a sudden twinge of elated anticipation, damped almost as soon as he felt it. Jess Marvell knew him under a couple of names, but not as Cole Brandon, so the letter could not be from her.

He opened the bank's envelope and took the letter out. He did not have to open it to know the sender. He had often enough seen Krista's elegant handwriting, still angular from her childhood schooling in Germany.

Brandon supposed that the plant standing in a tub to the left of his overstuffed chair in the lobby of the hotel was some kind of palm, though it looked equally like a giant fern. The probable palm, the painted pillars, the opulent chairs and couches, and the brocaded fabrics draping the tall windows facing the street spoke of the hotel's aspirations to be classed with the great establishments of Europe and the East; the gleaming brass spittoon on the floor to his right acknowledged that this was, after all, Chicago.

He had walked back from the bank with Krista's letter unopened in his jacket pocket, not sure whether he was resisting eagerness to read it until he could do so at leisure or simply putting off something he did not care to face. Now, putting aside his reflections on the potted plant and the spittoon, he fetched the letter out, looked again at the address, wondering if he might have been mistaken about the handwriting, if some other German-educated person might have written him at the bank that few but Krista knew he used, then slit the flap with his thumbnail and drew the letter out. It was a single folded sheet, written on one side, with a neat "as ever, Krista" at the bottom.

As the clerk's comment had suggested, the date at the top of the page was three months and a week in the past. Brandon refolded the letter and considered returning it to the envelope unread and disposing of it. He had no idea of what Krista would want to say to him, but could not see that it would further his task; and he sensed that any close consideration of St. Louis and in particular of Krista Ostermann could very well cloud his vision of the trail he had to follow.

Brandon sighed irritably and unfolded the paper. Leaving a received letter unopened or an opened letter unread was as unlikely as leaving an itch unscratched; it might be a good idea, but it was outside the boundaries of human behavior.

My Dear Cole,

I write this because I must. I do not know where you are, or when if ever this will reach you, but I owe it to you and to myself to tell you how things stand with me.

You know as well as I do what might have been between us. I understand that you wanted to travel to ease the pain of Lieschen's dreadful death, and that anything else would have to wait until your return. But I do not know if you will return to St. Louis, or if you do, if your feeling for me will be what I thought it was.

Life must go on, yours and mine, and I cannot stay forever as I am. The business occupies me greatly—I now do the work of general manager as well as president, and even the old hands acknowledge that I am a fit successor to poor Papa!—but I feel more and more that I must join my life and work with another's to be complete. You and I would not assort very smoothly—you are thoughtful, I am ambitious—but oil and vinegar can blend very pleasingly. I believe that our feeling for each other would overcome our contrast. It always seemed to me that when I attended concerts with you and Lieschen that you and I saw the same things in the music, though I do not know about that. But if that is not to be, it is time for me to take another course—one that, you might say, goes with my "vinegar" side!

Dearest Cole, if you receive this within two months of the above date, please have the kindness to write me honestly of your thoughts and wishes; whatever they are, you can be sure I will respect them.

If I have no reply by then, I must assume that

there is no reason to keep me from doing what is left to me to do.

As ever,
Krista

Brandon refolded the letter and slipped it into its envelope, then slid it into a jacket pocket and stared at the rich cascades of fabric at the hotel's front windows and the shafts of late morning sun pouring through them and throwing gilt squares onto the plush carpet. Bright dots of dust danced in the slanting light, and he tried to follow them with his eyes to see if they formed any kind of pattern that made sense.

"Another course . . . 'vinegar' side . . ." That sounded as if she meant to sink herself into the task of running and expanding the Ostermann enterprises and give up on the idea of joining her "life and work with another's." Krista could do that, and enjoy it, he knew. August Ostermann had treated her in many ways like the son he had not been granted, and he had passed on to her his zest for the details of his trading and manufacturing companies and his skill in handling men and money. It had been his intention that she inherit his direction of them as well as a share of his ownership, but both of them had supposed that it would be an experienced woman in her forties or fifties who would receive that inheritance, not one still short of thirty. Even in Brandon's months of apathy after the killings at Mound Farm he had noticed how Krista had taken hold of the business and earned the respect of department heads and workers; and it seemed she had been going on in just that way.

She might after all find someone to partner, though Brandon could see that it would be difficult. St. Louis had lots of amiable, well-off young men, but those with the character to interest Krista already had substantial careers and would want a wife who would help them further such a career, not one who was probably more able and business-wise than they were. It was hard to imagine the man with whom Krista could have a happy marriage.

Excepting or not excepting you, Counselor? his interior cross-examiner asked.

It's only a month beyond what she said, Brandon thought. If I wrote today, there's a good chance she wouldn't have done anything yet that couldn't be undone, and . . .

You're not going to, are you, Counselor?

No.

Krista was an important part of his past, but definitely the past, not the future. During his hunt for the murderers of his family Krista had receded into the background of his awareness, and now that she was suddenly again, if only in the form of her letter, a here-and-now presence, Brandon saw that there was no way he was going to bring her into the forefront of his life, now or later. He could have loved Krista; in a way he did love her, but not in any way that would join them. Not that he was a candidate to join with anyone, unless and until Gren Kenneally and the last of his men were dead.

And if, and then? Would Cole Brandon be reborn in his own person, dispensing with the masks he had worn and the roles he had lived? Would he go back to Walsh's Row, to Lunsford Ahrens & Brandon and the comfortable, satisfying, sometimes entertaining practice of law in St. Louis, meeting Krista with brotherly affection? It somehow didn't seem likely.

For one thing, Jess Marvell didn't seem to have a place in such a life. . . .

Brandon rose from his chair, went into the comfortable dark room that housed the bar, and ordered a highball. The soda and ice were unaccustomed refinements, and the whiskey was a good deal smoother than what he had become used to in the saloons of half a dozen states and territories, and he savored the drink with a relish spiced by the knowledge that it and the other luxuries he was enjoying in Chicago would soon be over.

There was one other drinker at the bar, ten feet or so from Brandon, a burly, well-dressed man in his fifties who seemed to be absorbed in the balloon glass on the bar in front of him. Brandon glanced at him, then looked away quickly. The long nose and big ears would be enough identification for readers of the illustrated papers, but Brandon had, some time back, had a closer acquaintance with the man, knew him with certainty, and hoped the acquaintance was not to be renewed.

In a moment, though, he heard approaching steps on the carpeted floor, and a grating voice, stretching for cordiality, said, "Blake, isn't it?"

If you're going to be recognized, Counselor, at least it's by a man who calls you by the name you're using now. "Yes, Mr. Parker, Calvin Blake."

"Good," the man said. "I usually forget names and faces of people I don't need to know, so it's something remarkable that I've kept hold of yours."

For John B. Parker, dubbed by the papers the Killer Elephant of Wall Street, this comment amounted to effusive friendliness. A speculator who had rigged markets to his own great profit and the ruin of hundreds, a railroad builder who made more money out of the graft involved than from the lines themselves, Parker was as a rule imperious to the point of outright insult. Brandon had saved him from kidnapping and possible death over in Colorado some time ago but doubted this service had anything to do with his unusually warm manner. Jake Trexler, the railroad detective who had served as Parker's unwilling bodyguard, said that he went in fear of being garroted—a popular form of assault with many of those disemployed by the depression who had drifted into crime. Most people who knew John B. Parker felt that the fear was justified; almost anybody who found himself in Parker's vicinity with a strong cord handy would feel tempted to use it.

Since their encounter, Brandon had learned that Parker was one of those tied by blood and interest to the Kenneallys, a connection carefully concealed and, in fact, hardly ever called upon, since Parker had mastered the lesson that using the law's complexities and flexibility was more effective than outright fracture, and often no less lethal for the victims.

About the only thing Brandon could think of to John B. Parker's credit was that he had eased Jess Marvell's construction of Marvel Halls at stations on one of his railroads, and, as far as Brandon had heard, had dealt with her fairly.

"Reporter for some newspaper in Colorado, aren't you?" Parker said.

"Spargill *Chronicle,*" Brandon said, "but not anymore."

"On a Chicago paper?"

"Not writing now," Brandon said. "Selling."

Parker moved a step back, as if to make clear that he was not a prospective client for whatever Brandon's wares might turn out to be. "Insurance?"

"Windmills. I'm western Nebraska agent for the Nonpareil windmill, known for its patented directional vane."

"Huh," John B. Parker said. "Nonpareil better hope the vane ain't all that such a much, or someone'll step in and put it out cheaper and find a way to get around the patent or break it."

"That'd be pretty hard to do," Brandon said.

"I could do it," John B. Parker said. Brandon noticed that in addition to having taken to dressing almost sprucely and to addressing persons of little importance with something approaching courtesy, Parker had been professionally shaved and barbered, with his hair bushed out at the side so as to minimize the prominence of his ears. It was almost as if he were setting himself out to make a favorable impression, an idea those who knew him at all would find laughable.

Brandon looked more closely at the carefully arranged hair. It might have been the dim light in the bar, but John B. Parker's iron-gray hair seemed darker than it had back in Colorado—more a wrought-iron gray, as reporter Calvin Blake, who had a deplorable bent for clever writing, might have put it.

Added to everything else, dyeing the hair was conclusive. Nineteen to one, Brandon thought, Parker's got a woman or is after one. He speculated on what this inamorata might be like and settled on an opulently curved actress or dancer with a strong appreciation of champagne, oysters, and precious stones. Not a whore, but satisfyingly whorish—that would be John B. Parker's taste.

Brandon was surprised to find himself envying what he supposed to be Parker's libertine liaison; it would be nice to have a simple sexual arrangement with no emotional responsibilities and concerns, just a few financial ones. His celibacy since Elise's death had not been policy, but whenever opportunity and inclination had coincided there had been some good reason not to seize the occasion. Right now he could not remember what the good reasons had been and somewhat regretted that they had seemed so valid at the time.

"Those windmills, they are a great thing," John B. Parker said. "Here, Blake, your glass is empty, have another." Brandon stared as Parker directed the bartender to refill Brandon's glass and to give him another cognac. Amiability, hospitality . . . was Parker's light-o'-love a reverse Circe, turning a swine into a human being? And one with civilized tastes, too: Brandon recognized the cognac the bartender was pouring as a superb and subtle one.

"Windmills let men farm where they couldn't used to," John B. Parker said. "Farther west you go, the less rain you can count on. You'll see, Blake, what happens to the crops. Over near Omaha, wheat and corn higher than your head, but the closer you get to Colorado, the shorter they get, till waist-high's a pretty good showing, and some years less. Windmill water's the way around that, no doubt about it, so you're doing a public service."

"I hadn't looked at it that way," Brandon said.

"Don't," John B. Parker said. "Sell the damn things to make your commission. That way you'll be sure to do your best job. The farmers grow food to make money, I ship their stuff to make money, and that's how it all works. Now, if you get them to buy your windmills, they'll have more crops, the farmland'll look like a better proposition, and immigrants will come in to start new farms."

Brandon reviewed what he knew of the railroad land grant laws and their results. "And if they want to be close to the railroad for shipping, they'll buy that farmland from the land the railroad holds."

"Not to mention buying their passage out there," John P. Parker said cheerfully. "I tell you, Blake, everywhere you look in the West, even with the depression, there's money to be squeezed out, like a sponge that's been soaking up sweet water for a month. You just have to touch it and hold your cup underneath. You're getting in at the right time."

He sipped his brandy. "This is good stuff. I mainly like whiskey, but this has as much of a jolt, and there's half a dozen flavors in it to get your tongue around. Man in St. Louis put me on to it; some of those Germans there know all there is to be known about good liquor. You know St. Louis, Blake?"

"Not lately," Brandon said.

4

"Congratulations, Calvin," Ralph Catesby said. "Here is your stuff. Pad of order forms, with the terms and conditions printed on each and every one, to be made out in three copies as I told you. Pad of telegraph forms for faster action if the customer's inclined, though full order form's got to be sent on anyhow. Prints of original patent drawings of the Catesby vane and the Wheeler mill—those are meant for regional or district offices, but they'll make a great impression when you roll 'em out on some farmer's kitchen table."

Catesby handed over the rolled drawings, carefully tied with cloth tape, with the air of an emperor bestowing the baton of office on a field marshal. Brandon took them, reflecting that nobody had called him "Calvin" during his previous run as Blake and hoping that no one would again.

"Full instructions on installation of mill and erection of supporting tower," Ralph Catesby continued. "That way they can have the tower ready when the mill gets there and be pumping water two hours after the crate's opened; has a wonderful effect when it happens that fast. Copy of owner's instructions, so's they can see what they have to do to keep the mill oiled and working and get in whatever tools they need. Don't let them borrow your copy to study, though, for they'll lose it or drop it where cows or pigs have been. They can wait till they get their own along with the mill."

Brandon hefted the stiffened cloth case that Catesby had provided for the documents and drawings and said, "Considering the merchandise, it's a light enough sample case."

Ralph Catesby exhaled slightly, just short of a resigned sigh. "I don't remember any salesman, here or with any other windmill company, that didn't make that joke. Maybe I've even made it myself. One of 'em laughed out of the other side of his face, though, for I had the notion to send him out with some models I made, one of the Nonpareil and one of the Halladay type, to show the customers the difference, and they were pretty cumbersome. But he run off with those as well as the money he collected, so he had the last laugh after all."

Brandon recalled the complicated mechanism that moved the Halladay mill's blades like shutters, altering its shape to respond to strong winds, and said. "The Halladay's so fancy I'd think a model of it would be hard to make work right; you'd have stop and fix it a lot of the time."

"Always," Ralph Catesby said with satisfaction.

Brandon left Catesby's office feeling that trading a thousand dollars for his new identity as an accredited Nonpareil representative was a hard bargain but one he could live with. Anyhow, if he left the firm's employ under any but catastrophic conditions, he could probably get it back. He doubted that his commissions on windmills sold would swell the company's profits enough to earn him any considerable dividend.

The sun was hot, and, contemplating the walk back to his hotel lugging the case, Brandon decided that a beer would be a good preparation for the journey.

The area abounded in saloons ranging from the seedy

to the sinister, which, none of them being more than a few years old, reminded Brandon of the sporting quarters of frontier towns rather than of a city with a good fifty years of history behind it.

A place identified simply as Dooley's looked acceptable, and he stepped inside. There were half a dozen men at the bar, none of them singing, shouting, arguing, or fighting, so it would do for a fast, quiet drink as well as the hotel would have—better, as the hotel bar offered the chance of meeting John B. Parker again. The changes in Parker were interesting to consider, but not interesting enough to bring Brandon to associate with him willingly.

When his beer came it was not up to Dolph Busch's St. Louis standard, but good enough. Parker's mention of St. Louis had pretty much ended their conversation yesterday, as Brandon was disinclined to talk or even think about the city he had left and the life he had left. Parker had been right, though, about some of St. Louis's Germans being connoisseurs of good drink as well as food; Elise's cousin Fredl could go on for hours about Bordeaux chateaux, the great pre–Phylloxera vintages, and the contrasting virtues and vices of all the varieties of brandy. . . .

Brandon switched his train of thought from a track he had not meant it to travel and let the conversation between the young bartender and a client at the far end of the bar drift to him.

"Now," the bartender said, "what's a hundred years, to be cellybratin' it so fierce? In the old country it's an eyeblink. We don't notice a insult for two cinturies, nor forget it in ten. I'm for anything that'll give business a lift, but a cinteenery's flimsy doins for the job. They don't come along often enough."

"There'll be stuff as what's older'n a hundrit years, older'n any old country whatevers, not excluding Chiny and Ur of the Chaldees, to be seen at Philadelphy." Brandon looked up sharply at the sound of the grating voice, penetrating as that of an unoiled gate hinge.

"A bit of bone from Adam wud it be, like a saint's relic?" the bartender said sardonically.

"Bone, but not jist a bit, and not from Adam," the customer said. "Monsters as walked the earth before Adam, and their bones buried and peterfried into rock, and now dug up by long-headed perfessors to be haywired together and showed at the Exposition as they was in life, only withouten the skin and such."

"So low in flesh, so high in bone, like the song says, is that it?" the bartender said. "Now, I'm obliged to tell you, it's the house rule that when the customer gits to talkin' of monsters and spiders an' that class of creature, it's best to stop servin' him, as . . ."

Brandon picked up his beer and moved swiftly down the bar. Past experience suggested that the saloon was in imminent danger of suffering damage as extreme as its predecessor had sustained from the Fire: If the customer was who he was certain it was, he was inclined to devastate any establishment that irritated him, and he found being refused drink service irritating beyond measure.

"Hello, there!" Brandon said heartily as he approached what appeared to be an untidy bundle of leather topped with an almost shapeless broad-brimmed hat leaning up against the bar. "Calvin Blake, remember me? Last I saw you, you were going to start guiding a bunch of scientists hunting for dinosaur bones—how did that go?"

"Fine, as I was tellin' Marty here," the customer said, his seamed face rearranging itself into a grin. "Ned Norland, as you'll recall." Brandon nodded; the reintroductions had been performed without the rudeness of addressing someone outright by a name that might not be in current use. Even in a place like Dooley's, men used to the ways of the frontier would follow established etiquette.

"Like dragons, bigger than houses, some of those dinosaurs, that's what I've heard," Brandon said.

The bartender was impressed. "It's the straight goods, then, that this gintleman is dealin' in real monster bones, to be showed at the Cintinnery Exposition?"

"Absolutely, a wonder of the age, written up extensively in *Scientific American* and *Leslie's*. Mr. Norland's known as one of the first experts on them," Brandon said. He considered that Ned Norland could be stuffed and mounted and displayed as an ancient monster himself, at least as dangerous as any giant lizard—and had imparted some of that dangerousness to Brandon, which was one reason Brandon was alive today. He turned to Norland and said, "Here, Norland, what're you drinking?"

"Rye whiskey," Norland said. "Marty, bottle, two glasses, the which me and Mr. Blake will disport ourselves with whilst conversationin' at yonder table by the wall. That all right with you?" He cocked an appraising eye at the mirror behind the bar.

"Surest thing ever," the bartender said, reaching for the bottle and glasses, cheerfully unaware of the destruction he had nearly loosed. "Customers is free to see all the real monsters they wants. It's the imaginary ones that makes the throuble."

At the table Ned Norland plied Brandon with tales of his adventures leading the dinosaur-hunting expedition in Arizona. "I been goin' over this country fer a elephant's years, Blake, and I never knew nothin' about it 'cept how to stay alive in it, take some pelts, make money tradin', hunt buffler and b'ar and antelope and all the fowls of the air, drive a train of freight wagons acrost it, fight the crafty Injun, and hump whatever prime women was persuadable to it, but wagh! This child didn't know nothin'! Them perfessors showed me how as all them badlands useter be ocean bottoms, then dry land, then ocean bottoms ag'in, with whatas lived and crawled around betweentimes gettin' covered over with mud and turned to stone."

Ned Norland refilled his glass and went a good way

toward re-emptying it with a gulp. "They showed me them mesas with all the layers in them, like the fancy drinks they has in New Orleans, pussycuffs or what, and tolt me how many thousands of years went into each inch of each layer. And I minded me of the times I seen the Canyon of the Arizony that's a mile down from the top to the river, that's got them same kind of rock layers, and I figure there ain't enough folks in the country to hand-count the years that took. Like the bar dick said, a century don't seem like much alongside that."

"Gives you a kind of awed feeling?" Brandon said.

"Some. But mainly the feelin' that sixtywhat ain't much out of the cradle, so this child has got a lot of women to pleasure still, the which I means to keep at till it's my time to turn to stone. Maybe after, dependin' where the turnin' to stone starts."

"Any trouble while you were at it? Digging for the dinosaurs, that is," Brandon said. "Indians, robbers?"

"Nope. Perfessors and preachers, though, the which is worse."

Ned Norland explained that rival scientists from a university competing for paleontological prestige with the institution sponsoring the expedition he was guiding had conducted a kind of guerrilla campaign. "When we got to the nearest to where we was to dig it turned out these fellers had hired off all our crew, so's we had to scratch up a new bunch. And they got a lease on a place we'd meant to dig in, which was a boon and blessin' to us, since the place we had to fall back on turnt out to give us a big spike-back critter like nobody'd seen."

"I sort of had the idea that scientists didn't get into those kinds of fights," Brandon said. "Above it all."

"Nobody ain't above nothin' when somethin' gits in the way of what somebody wants," Ned Norland said. "True fer me, true fer you if you'll look at the proposition honest. Your perfessor ain't no different, nor neither ain't your preacher. There was one that heared of what we was up to and come out to castigate and reprehend

32

us, sayin' as we was doin' the devil's work, confusin' the faithful by pretendin' as these bones we was diggin' up was millions of years old, whilst the Good Book lays it out that Creationing was done about seven thousand years back, if you count up all the begats and pedigreein' in Genesis."

"How'd the professors take that?" Brandon asked.

"Why, they explained that the Bible weren't to be taken literately, and the preacher comminated them with threats of the lake of brimstone. And then they said as how these critters had ruled the roost for a hundrit times as long as it's been since there was people at all, and he called down plagues and botches of Egypt on 'em. And they tolt him that some of them old-time reptiles turnt into kinder like rats, and the rats by'n' by turnt into monkeys and then the monkeys into men, and he foamed at the mouth and spoke in tongues and fell onto the floor in a fit. And then he went away and tried to git some missionaried Injuns to massacree us for blaspheming."

"I see they didn't," Brandon said. "They make a try?"

"Naw," Ned Norland said. "When they took it in that we was communin' with stone dragons they beat up the preacher some severe and came to work for us, figuring the sarpints was bigger medicine than what the missionaries had on offer."

"At least they didn't scalp him," Brandon said after a moment's absorption of the story, just absurd enough to be perhaps true.

"Missionarying takes a while to fade out, like sunburn," Ned Norland said. "I expect there'll be more like the preacher at the Exposition, but the guards'll likely move 'em on. I'm goin' to Philadelphy tomorrer with the last shipment of bones; rest of 'em's already there, and the perfessers is fittin' 'em together to edificate and terrify the populace when the show opens." He looked at Brandon. "But you ain't on your way to Philadelphy, I don't s'pose, though it's unexpectin' t' see you here. Last we met, I said as how I'd do my brag on lizard diggin' when we crossed trails ag'in, and you'd tell me how many Kenneallys you'd counted coup on. I done my end, for fair, and now it's your turn."

Brandon realized that one thing he had been feeling since he heard Ned Norland's voice down the bar was relief. Norland was the only man who knew everything of his mission—had been with him at Mound Farm at the first kill that had led to the rest. The tong lord Tsai Wang in San Francisco and a few of the shadowy Kenneallys and Kenneally connections had some knowledge of it, but Norland was part of it and had trained Brandon in the arts of hunting and tracking as best he could, pointing out that hunting men and hunting animals were not so different. Norland was the only person in the world with whom Brandon did not have to feel guarded in some way—even Jess Marvell was not allowed to know what work he was about—and talking with him was like taking off tight boots after a twenty-mile walk.

"Three since I saw you," he said. "One killed alongside me in a fight before I knew who he was, one chewed up by a steamer's paddle wheel at sea, one I shot while he was shooting at me. That leaves five, counting Gren."

Ned Norland whistled. "Middlin' brisk work. Hum, last time I seed you you weren't sure of the count, how many'd been in at the start."

"I got an inventory." Brandon explained about the assistance the Kenneally-connected judge had provided, and the bizarre reasons for it.

"Now, that is a picture," Ned Norland said. "One bunch of Kenneallys robbin' and plunderin' straightforward like, and another bunch of 'em doin' much the same and bein' respected and looked up to for it."

He tilted the whiskey bottle to pour a tablespoonful into Brandon's glass and emptied the rest of its contents into his own. "A dreadful and unpleasin' prospect, a fambly of thieves, pickpockets, and garroters exertin' their baneful influence along and acrost this fair land."

He gulped at the whiskey and said, "What keeps it from bein' outright discouragin' is that the bankers and politicians that ain't Kenneallys seems to be operatin' along the same lines, so it don't make that much of a difference. Now, for why you's in Chicago and not out where your men are likely to be?"

Brandon explained the combination of vague clues and hunches that led him to think that the farmlands of western Nebraska were the best place to try. "It don't seem much to go on," he said, "but you always taught me to follow instinct, and mine's pointing me there."

Ned Norland nodded. "Game you're after, you ain't gonna find it by the reg'lar ways. Wagh! If'n I hadn't turnt off my brains and let my guts tell me what to do more times'n not, I'd been scalped or a pauper or both back in Andy Jackson's time. You still got that old-time coin you dug out of the mound when we planted that feller?"

Brandon felt the worn disk of metal in his pocket and nodded.

"Good," Ned Norland said. "I tolt you before, that's powerful medicine, and you best pay it mind whenas it's got somethin' to tell you. But Chicago ain't a stopover between Nebrasky and anyplace you been so far, so that query is still lyin' out flat on the plate and no fork dug into it as yet."

Brandon explained the Nonpareil scheme and went so far as to draw out the patent drawings and show them to Norland. "I've been a lot of things so far," he said, "but this job looks like it might be interesting on its own. You know, these damn machines are fascinating."

"Farms and farm machines and windmills is makin' the West over into Ohio or New York State," Ned Norland said. "They is growin' acrost the prairie like the mange. When I was a kit, wasn't nothin' but prairie on the prairie, mountains in the mountains, and some Injuns and critters makin' use of 'em without leavin' a dent nor a scratch that you could notice. It's progress, like what's on show at the Exposition, and I cain't argue ag'inst it, I expect, but I don't keer for it. But you want to watch out whiles as you're out spreadin' the mange."

He looked hard at Brandon. "Windmills and the other stuff you done, they's the masks you got to wear so's them you're trackin' won't see your true face. Watch out you don't wear a mask so tight and so long that whenas you take it off the face underneath is the same as the mask."

5

After what seemed an interminable time traveling across a table-flat landscape, varying as to what was covering it from tough, ancient prairie grass to the fresh green of new crops, the low bluffs and modestly rolling hills marking where the prairie started to yield to the high plains seemed to Brandon as dramatic and inspiriting as the Alps.

Instead of lying flat on the track bed like a silhouette, the shadow of the car flexed and curved as it rode up a suddenly appearing embankment, then down again as it passed. He began to see trees, mostly cottonwood, some elms and willows. A pair of houses slid by the window, then a few more, and a dirt road paralleling the track became evident; the train whistled and slowed.

Like any traveler on a journey not made before, Brandon knew that this stop was not his but could not resist making sure that his valise was in place on the overhead rack, in case he had dozed through a stop and this really was Bigsbee.

"Platteville! Stop's Platteville!" the conductor called, and Brandon relaxed. The county seat, Bigsbee an hour's ride down the line. The train shuddered to a halt, with its usual spiteful jerk that tested the strength of the passengers' necks. A neater-looking place than most towns Brandon had seen in the West, more a kind of Ohio look, as Ned Norland had complained, he saw as he surveyed the area around the station from his window. Maybe farm-country towns tended to be more orderly than places tied to the cattle trade.

The stores and businesses seemed in good repair, and there were no saloons or evident brothels in view of the station, so civic self-respect seemed to be important. But as Brandon continued to survey the scene it seemed to fade slightly, as if a film of dust had been deposited on it. For a moment he could not understand why, then he saw it. A town like this, he thought, at train time should have a bustle around the station, arriving and departing passengers and the simply curious; and there should be a gaggle of customers for the stores, loading up buggies with purchases or carrying parcels. The street and station platform were by no means deserted, but there were far fewer than half the people he would have expected to see. Maybe there was some important event going on in town that had drawn everyone there. More likely it was that the depression had bitten even deeper here than in other places he'd been. As he had thought on his way to Chicago, this region wasn't going to be aswarm with customers demanding Nonpareil windmills, no matter how much they might need them.

Of course, the windmill market was not his main concern. Bigsbee offered a better reason for serving as his headquarters. One of the entries on the list the judge had given him—one of the four not yet crossed off—was

Dick the Farmer, also Neb, no last name known. Assoc. of GK only for CRI&P robbery. Average appearance, no distinguishing scars, &c. Said to be knowledgeable about agriculture, hence nickname.

Not much to go on, but Brandon had had a report from Jess Marvell and Rush Dailey that a man who might be this Dick the Farmer was said to be on his way from Colorado to somewhere in western Nebraska, which he proclaimed to be the richest farmland in the world. Bigsbee was one of the first farm communities a man coming from Colorado would fetch up at—west of there was traditionally cattle country, and the cattlemen were still holding their own against the advance of the plowmen—and so it would be somewhat better than any other place to start looking for him.

By now Brandon was used to allowing destiny or chance a major role in his quest. Ned Norland had said a long time back that men's lives ran on courses, like tracks, and that if the tracks were meant to intersect, they would. Often enough Brandon had put himself where a hunch, or even an obscure sign from the old Indian coin he carried, seemed to indicate the encounter he sought. It wasn't much of a way for a rational modern man in the last quarter of the nineteenth century to act, but, he reflected, blood vengeance wasn't all that modern and rational either. Shakespeare and Kyd and those playwrights knew all about it, and so had men all the way back to the Bible and before.

The stretch of line between Platteville and Bigsbee showed a gratifying variety of landscape and a twisting creek with chalk bluffs that seemed to flirt with the tracks, twisting away from them, then running alongside for a stretch. The creek looked cool and comfortable, and like a place a man could walk, fish, or just laze on the bank or in a boat. A man who didn't have the job of hunting down and killing five other men, anyhow . . .

Far more rarely than in the flatter, lusher eastern reaches of the state, farms appeared, both nearby and in the distance, patches of bright green and bare brown earth, animals and buildings turned toy-size by distance. Some distance out of Platteville they disappeared altogether, and the land was as it had been before the settlers, if you looked past the cinders and pebbles of the track bed and ignored the steady flicker of telegraph poles.

When farms—none of them with windmills—once

more broke the wilderness prospect, Brandon knew that Bigsbee was not far ahead; farmers had to be reasonably near a railroad stop if they were to have any chance of getting their crops to where they could be sold.

Confirming this, a group of grain elevators loomed on one side of the train and slid by; then the river, which had been keeping company with the train, now seemed to wish to commit suicide and threw itself under the engine, but it reappeared unharmed at the other side of the tracks as the train bumped over a bridge and slowed for its approach to the station.

"*Bigs*bee, all passengers for Bigsbee!" the conductor said, with a forced heartiness that suggested that Bigsbee was one of the places that made a man glad to keep traveling on.

Brandon gathered his valise and stepped onto the station platform. Bigsbee was like a pocket Platteville: same sorts of stores and businesses, but fewer, and the buildings lower; same underpopulated streets and air of weariness. He knew that the effects of the depression had been compounded by the ravages of grasshoppers for the last few years, and that the farmers were feeling, if not desperate, pretty battered. Between the cars he caught sight of the creek, rippling in the sun at the other side of the tracks, providing a contrasting and welcome note of liveliness.

He did not expect to have to ask the way to the Station Hotel, which a surprisingly well-informed railroad clerk in Chicago had told him was the principal and only hotel in Bigsbee; and indeed it was across the street from the station.

The locomotive, having paused for fifteen seconds, exhaling impatiently, like a mastiff pulling at the leash, waited until it was clear that the conductor's cry of "Bw*oar*art! Aw*boart!*" had produced no passengers, then flexed its drivers, heaved into motion, and drew the train out of the station.

Brandon hoisted his valise and walked toward the hotel. The new suit he had bought in Chicago, in deference to his standing as a representative of Nonpareil, felt stiff and tight, and what had seemed up-to-date there seemed over-fancy here.

Makes me look like a damn traveling salesman, he told himself. It took a couple of seconds for him to realize what he had silently said, and to grin.

Well, you've been traveling enough, Counselor; what is it you've been selling? Death insurance, maybe. Instant end to your troubles. Just consult Cole Brandon and his capable assistant Calvin Blake, not to mention Chuck Brooks, Carter Bane, and the rest, and peace of mind will be yours. If you don't believe in Hell and damnation, anyhow. Only Gren Kenneally and the other four are eligible for this special offer; don't wait.

Brandon lay on the bed in his room at the Station Hotel and looked at the ceiling. Certainly he'd seen as many hotel rooms and boardinghouse rooms and ceilings as any traveling salesman. Going to sleep looking up at the canvas top of the chuck wagon on the Circle C drive had been about the biggest change of sleeping quarters scenery he had had since he left St. Louis. Weeks on the trail, that had been, and four people dead along the way, one of them the man he'd been after, so it had been worthwhile.

The ceiling in the Station Hotel room was plain plaster, not stamped tin like many of the places that aspired to elegance, and not the underside of the roof rafters, like the many more that had never entertained the concept. Like any apparently plain surface, a lake or a prairie, it developed features, slowly, as you looked at it, something like the way a photographer's glass plate did.

Furrows, dips, and cracks in the plaster arranged themselves into patterns . . . perhaps sections of a map that might join together to show an unknown territory? That long line twisted like a river, and the shadows of a couple of shallow depressions toward the window might mark lakes.

Not a map, he suddenly saw. The descending sun was

level with the window now, and every irregularity in the ceiling cast erratic, sharp shadows. For a moment he saw what could have been the outline of a four-footed creature with a sharp muzzle; then the sun dipped behind a building across the alley, and the whole ceiling was lost in featureless dimness.

He rooted in his pocket and came out with the coin. It had clinked against his shovel that midnight at Mound Farm when he and Ned Norland dug the grave for the first of Gren Kenneally's men to die, and Norland had claimed that it was meant for him to find and take, one of those accidents that are not really accidents.

He studied the worn disk, tracing on one side the blurred figure of the predatory beast that looked so like what he had just seemed to have seen on the ceiling, and on the other the raised ridge around the edge that resolved, when you looked long enough, into the image of a snake with its tail in its mouth. Chief Atichke in New Mexico knew those signs and told Brandon that the snake was swallowing itself or giving birth to itself; either way, it meant that what had been was changing to what would be, and that the holder of the coin had a task that must be seen to. The wolf on the other side of the coin told of the nature of the task: to hunt and kill.

Brandon returned the coin to his pocket and sat up on the edge of the bed. He set his valise beside him, opened it, and pulled out his arsenal. This consisted of an authoritative .38 revolver, once the property of a gambler who had gambled on not needing to draw it and lost, and a single-shot .30-caliber pistol, also part of the gambler's estate. This last came with a spring mechanism that could deliver it from a hiding place in the sleeve into the palm of the hand with an unobtrusive squeeze of the arm. Brandon had practiced the maneuver a few times but had never had occasion to put it to practical use. The main virtue of the smaller weapon was that it could nestle unnoticed in his vest, even with a suit as tight as his new one. The .38, unfortunately, would be obvious however he carried it, and this did not seem like a town where men habitually carried sidearms—certainly not windmill salesmen fresh from Chicago.

He tucked the single-shot pistol into the pocket of his vest, draped over the back of the chair next to the nightstand. It might be a long time before he came across the man he was hunting. It could also happen the moment he stepped out into the street. Preparing for the second possibility was the way to stay alive.

"It's good of you to pay me a call, Mr. Blake," Simon Rattner said. "There's not much business in Bigsbee now, and a new face in town makes a change in the day. But I don't see what you want of me. I assume you don't want a loan to set yourself up in the windmill business, for you're already in it."

He looked inquiringly at Brandon across his oak desk, the principal piece of furniture in the large, airy room that took up the rear of the bank building. The president of the Agriculturists & Commercial Bank was a broad-faced man of about fifty whose air of mild melancholy had lightened a little at Brandon's knock and request for a conversation. He wore a shabby suit that made Brandon feel that his own belonged back on a haberdasher's dummy, not in this hardscrabble town.

"No, no," Brandon said. "No business at all, really. But I hoped I could tell you what I'm here to do, get some notions from you on how to go about it."

"Well, you know your business a great deal better than I do," Rattner said, with considerably less truth than he could imagine, "so I can't imagine what use I could be."

"The whole trade of the town comes through the bank, one way or another," Brandon said. "And that includes the farmers. They may have homesteaded the land cheap and started out in sod shanties they dug out of the ground, but they likely had to borrow money for equipment and seed, and even if they didn't, at least they keep the money their crops bring in the bank. The way things are, there's probably hardly one of 'em that doesn't have some kind of loan running with you."

At Simon Rattner's nod he continued, "So you know better than anyone who's in a position to make the kind of investment a windmill requires. You can tell me which of the farmers it makes sense to call on, for their benefit and mine. And the bank's, of course, for when they get the mill and the water gets to pumping they'll have crops like never before, and they'll pay off their loans and increase their business with the bank."

"My," Simon Rattner said, "you make it seem like one of those articles in the magazines about how the great cycle of trade benefits everybody. They usually have engravings of fellows in work clothes shaking hands with fellows in tailcoats, and both of 'em smiling from ear to ear. What they don't show is the fellows in tailcoats' hands in the others' pockets."

As it was from such an article, clipped and handed to him for study by Ralph Catesby, that Brandon had lifted his line of argument, he kept silent.

"What it amounts to," Rattner said with friendly amusement, "is, you'd like me to save you some work."

"Yes," Brandon said, there being no use in denying it. "But it means saving your customers some trouble, too. I mean, there's no use me doing a bang-up job of selling Nonpareil's top model to a poor fellow that can't afford it, no matter that it might be the saving of his farm."

Simon Rattner was silent for a moment as he looked at Brandon. "There's enough of those, God knows. . . . And, though you didn't say it, you've mousetrapped me very nicely into saying it myself: If he loses the farm, I lose whatever I've lent him, and if there's enough of that, the bank's got a lot of empty farms and not much money. So what you expect me to do is work out which farmers I can lend money to buy one of your windmills so I can get back that loan and their outstanding ones. And now that you've brought it up, I don't see any way out of at least looking into it. You're shrewd to have worked that out, Mr. Blake."

Brandon, fascinated by the evolution of an idea in

whose birth he had not had the slightest conscious role, said, "Nice of you to say so."

"Well," Rattner said, "I'd better have a look at your windmills so I can see what I'm expected to finance. Brought your sample case with you, have you?" He blinked at Brandon and quickly said, "Sorry, I imagine men in your line hear that joke all the time and get pretty tired of it."

"You get so you don't mind," Brandon said. "What I do have is these full and complete patent drawings, which, if you'll find some books or what to hold the corners down, I will unroll on your desk and explain to you why the Nonpareil has no equal in its field. The patent vane . . ."

6

"You certainly know your goods, Mr. Blake," Simon Rattner said after Brandon had spun his store of knowledge of the Nonpareil and windmills in general out to fifteen minutes, fully twelve more than he would have thought possible. "Tomorrow I'll give you a list of men you can feel free to encourage to come to me for the money to buy one of your windmills. Also the ones you might as well not go near, for they don't have it and won't get it from me or anybody, being strangers to the idea of paying for anything."

He pulled a massive watch from his vest pocket and consulted it. "I take a cup of coffee most mornings about this time," he said. "Edwards the groceryman keeps a pot going in his back room, and me and some of the men in town like to drop in and talk about what's going on. Doesn't interfere with business much, damn it. You want to come along? The fellows'll be interested in the mills, would be in anything that looked to promote trade a little. Also, one or two of them might be interested in lending a farmer money privately, which would ease things for me if the idea takes hold."

At Brandon's agreement he stood up, took a parcel

wrapped in brown paper from the top of a safe against the wall, and escorted Brandon from the building. They walked down the street, which, though unpaved, seemed less broken and rutted than one might expect. Brandon thought that it was probably because of lack of business activity, with its concomitant traffic of road-abusing hooves and wheels, rather than efficient municipal maintenance. He also realized that, presumably for the same reason, Bigsbee smelled less of horse droppings than almost any place he had been in.

"I need to get some shoes resoled," Rattner said, holding up the parcel he had taken from his office. "All right to stop in here for a minute?"

As they were outside a frame building with a sign over the door reading ANGELO ANTONELLI, SHOEMAKER & REPAIRS, the request seemed reasonable. "Sure," Brandon said.

They stepped inside the store, and a swarthy, curly-haired young man looked up from a shoe repair in progress on the last he straddled, in appearance practically a stage Italian except for an air of stern melancholy that clouded what looked to be a normally lively countenance.

"Afternoon, Angelo," the banker said.

"Gude afternyune, Mr. Rattner," the shoemaker said in a singsong tone that drew Brandon's sharp attention.

"Here's these," Rattner said, opening the parcel on the counter. "Think you can get some new soles to hold on 'em?"

"Ay resole 'em like nyeu," Antonelli said after a quick but thorough inspection.

"Day after tomorrow, maybe?"

"Yah, sure," Antonelli said.

As Brandon and Rattner left the store the shoemaker returned to his work; an apparent missed stroke of his hammer produced a vexed "Uffda!"

Rattner gave Brandon a sidelong glance as they walked along the street. "There is a strange story there, Blake."

"There would have to be," Brandon said.

47

The story was that Antonelli had come from Italy as a youth nearly ten years ago and had, by some shifts he could not remember, made his way across country to one of the earliest settlements in mid–Nebraska. Knowing only his own language, he was resolved to acquire that of his new country and devoted himself to mastering it and determinedly forgetting his own. He did so and, gaining proficiency in the cobbler's trade, earned a respected place in the community.

"Trouble was, it was a place called New Hjemboe, settled totally by folks from Norway that spoke only Norwegian amongst themselves and not a word of English, so that was what Antonelli learned, though not knowing it. Wasn't till he was a Norsky in everything but looks that some drummer come through and let him know there how things were in the rest of America. He saw fast enough that he could get along in New Hjemboe and in parts of Minnesota with what he had, but not many places else, so he pulled stakes and fetched up here a year or so back, and he's trying to get easy with English, talk more like the rest of us."

"Look like he's making progress at it?"

"Yah sure," Rattner said.

There were no farmers in the group in the back room of Edwards's store, but there were a few ex-farmers among them, and none whose fortunes did not ride directly on those of the farmers around Bigsbee. The town had come into being to serve the farms, or rather the town and the farms had helped bring each other into being. As soon as the railroad had come through and a station was established, farming the land nearby became a paying proposition, and farmers homesteaded; the rudimentary settlement around the town sprouted a bank and stores to serve the farmers; with such facilities, the number of farms increased, and the town's business expanded accordingly. But, as Simon Rattner had said of optimistic presentations of the workings of business, the simplified picture didn't tell everything, and many farmers had not been able to make a go of it.

"I went busted farming," Danby the barber and a member of the town council told Brandon. "Grasshoppers, mostly. My place was some north and west of here, and it didn't have water on it, and none of your windmills to make up for it, so the 'hoppers got me worse than some. When they'd gone by I looked at that ground, mowed bare as an egg, and I figured it for a sign I should go in for shaving and haircutting."

"Lot of us left our trades in the East and came out here to farm," Edwards said. "I figured I knew all about vegetables from years of grocerying, and the handbills the railroad sent around made it look like a man could come out here, plant what he liked, and have the hired men pick it and send it off to market by fast express trains while he sat on a porch rocker and counted the proceeds. I didn't expect it would be that easy, only about half so, but it was nowhere near. All the same, I managed to grow something, even with the grasshoppers, but the railroad jumped the grain elevator charges and freight rates and cleared whatever profit there was to it. So I gave it up and went back to selling produce instead of raising it."

"And there's some that came from the other direction," said Swanson, the photographer and sign painter. "Fellows that got tired of the cattle business west of here or couldn't get work in it anymore and thought farming would be steadier. Some of 'em are doing well enough— getting by, anyhow, farming or working as hired hands— and others aren't, and they hang around the north edge of town, living by scrounging and God knows how."

"Come November, there better be a change," Danby said. "I see in the papers that the Prohibition Party and the Greenback Party just had conventions. I like a drink as well as the next man, and I don't know how whatever the Greenbackers want would work, but if either of 'em can turn things around, they're welcome to my vote."

"The Grange'll have a voice come election time," Kingslake, the editor, publisher, and chief writer of the Bigsbee *Bee,* said. "They'll give John B. Parker and the other railroad buzzards something that'll stick in their gullets. What's left after the grain elevators goes on the train with the freight rates."

"Maybe Parker and them," Geary, the gents' and ladies' outfitter, said. "But the Grange or the Prohibs or the Greenbackers can't none of 'em do anything about the grasshoppers if they come back this year."

"Some signs they won't," someone said.

"If they do, we ought to call in Febold Feboldson," Edwards said.

The crowd looked expectantly toward Brandon. He recognized that, as the newcomer, he was expected to prod Edwards along the way on what seemed to be a welcome diversion from contemplating the human and insect predators threatening them. "Who's Febold Feboldson?"

"The first white settler in Nebraska Territory," Edwards said solemnly. "Febold was as strong as they come, times ten—still is, for a fact. The year it was so cold the snow petrified and stayed on the ground all summer so's the emigrant trains couldn't get through, it was Febold had the idea to go to Death Valley, where the sand never gets below burning, and bring cartloads of it back to spread on the snow, which is why the prairies are so hot in summer nowadays. And when there wasn't any wood for fence posts out on the prairie, Febold dug post holes in the fall, and when they froze hard in winter dug 'em up and varnished 'em and sold 'em as red cedar. I expect Febold would just stand up in front of those grasshopper clouds and dast 'em to come on and swallow 'em as they came."

"And belch out bug dust on John B. Parker," someone said.

"I think he'd take one of those frozen post holes and push it up John B. Parker till it comes out of his mouth," Danby said.

If John B. Parker ever came to town, Brandon thought, a visit to Danby for a shave should remove his fear of being garroted. After Danby had done what he could with a razor there would be little for a garroter to work on.

Brandon left Simon Rattner at the door of Edwards's store and headed back toward the hotel. He turned the conversation over in his mind and thought that he had been accepted in a friendly enough way by the local businessmen, in spite of his suit, which, in contrast to their casual attire—Rattner was the best-dressed of the crowd—seemed to him something like the costume of a dude in some melodrama of mythical Wild West.

As he approached an alley between two buildings he got a rank whiff that reminded him of a bear den he had found as a boy in Missouri, foul and menacing, then stopped and found himself confronting a different member of the cast of a Wild West show: the stage bad man, huge, with matted hair and beard, dressed in ragged, greasy clothes, with staring, bloodshot eyes.

What was especially disconcerting was the impression of power and brutal intelligence that the man radiated along with his stench. This was no ordinary small-town drunken bully, though he seemed drunk and in a bullying frame of mind, and Brandon wondered if he could be the man he had come to Bigsbee to find. He looked capable of doing anything Gren Kenneally might suggest, but that was nowhere nearly enough to go on.

"Ain't you the pretty little goddamn dude, though?" the man said, adding a gust of whiskey fumes to the acrid miasma around him. "Them pipestem pants don't look like they got room for a pair o' balls in 'em, but they fit you jist right anyhow, don't they, Mary-boy?"

The trousers in fact fit tighter than Brandon found comfortable, and he agreed with the basic opinion the drunk expressed, but that had no bearing on the current situation. The extreme borders of his vision gave him an impression of figures standing quite still, including the men he had just left at Edwards's store, and nobody moving in his direction. No prospect, then, of outraged citizens rushing to aid a menaced stranger, assuming that the menace was real.

The man moved closer to Brandon, massive belly almost touching his chest, and glared redly down at him. "B'lieve I'll peel them pants off'n you an' see if you's gelded to make 'em fit. If you ain't, why, here's the man that can do the job, one bite, the which I don't mind a-doing of none. Dudes in fancy suits eats up the poor man worse'n grasshoppers, an' don't do to git treated no better!"

The man began to spread his arms, and Brandon knew that once in that grip his ribs and backbone were in serious hazard. A quick leap backward and a good sprint down the street would probably solve the problem with the least disturbance and peril. It would also allow him to wind up his business in Bigsbee and move on that very day, since the townsmen and farmers, though tamer than miners and cowboys, were still westerners, and would not respect a man who turned and ran. Buying a windmill should have nothing to do with how much sand the man who sold it had in his craw, but nobody would feel comfortable talking to someone who lacked it.

Ned Norland had had some interesting tips and reminiscences on close-quarters combat. A lot of them had to do with the jaw action necessary to detach most of an opponent's ear or nose, but there was at least one that seemed applicable right now.

Brandon bunched and stiffened the fingers of his left hand and drove them, tips first, into the man at what he hoped was the border between belly and ribs, bending his knees and striking upward to add force to the blow.

The man's face went blank, and his mouth and eyes opened wide. For several seconds he would be unable to breathe in or out if the blow had hit right, but Brandon was not inclined to be either merciful or leisurely. Before the bystanders could see what had happened he hit the man squarely in the gut, starting him folding like a

jointed ruler; then, as the staring face sank toward him,
he landed an uppercut to the jaw, jolting the man's head
back and sending him collapsing in a malodorous heap
onto the dirt-surfaced street.

Brandon stepped back, and three men from the group
of mesmerized onlookers came to life, darted over, and
half lifted, half rolled the unconscious man into the alley
from which he had emerged.

"His friends'll see to him when he comes to," Rattner
said as he came up to where Brandon stood breathing
heavily and deciding that on balance it had been better
not to whip out the .30 and shoot his assailant. Bigsbee
might view the response as extreme.

"They have practice with picking him up after doings
like this?" Brandon asked.

"Usually it's us picking up whoever tangled with him,"
Simon Rattner said.

"Police don't bother him?"

Rattner shook his head. "We have a chief and a
constable. That's all the town can afford—maybe a little
more than we can. Then this fellow—Jere Sublette his
name is—he drifted into town, and some like him, and
there's not much the two police can do short of shooting
him outright, and he's not killed or maimed anybody yet
or been proven to steal or such, so most folks just try to
stay out of his way."

"Ah, then . . ." Brandon said.

Simon Rattner nodded. "Yeah. You're the first I recollect to take Sublette on and whip him. I expect it'll get
you in to see about any farmer around that you want to,
since they'll want to hear the story and shake your hand.
You're a big man around here right now, Blake."

Big men stand out in a crowd, Brandon thought.
That's not what I'm after. But there's not much I can do
but let the story get cold and shrink down to my normal
size.

"Better you than me, though," Rattner said.
"Sublette's got the name of wanting an eye for an
eye—maybe a head for an eye, you might say—and for

having a long memory. Walk fast and look around often, that's what I'd advise from now on."

And carry a gun you can rely on. . . . Brandon resolved to drop in to Geary's outfitting store that afternoon and get a jacket capacious enough to look normal around Bigsbee—and to conceal the fact that its wearer was packing a .38 revolver.

7

These three—Swicegood, Harmon, and Bechtold—they ought to be able pay for one of your windmills, at least if you're doing it in installments," Simon Rattner said, tapping the first names on his list with his forefinger.

Brandon leaned back in the visitor's chair facing the desk, feeling more relaxed than he had yesterday. The jacket from Geary's fitted him more like a Mexican's poncho than a fashionable gent's pinch-back, but its plain cloth and loose fit sorted well enough with Rattner's suit. And he could be carrying two .45 "hoglegs" and a couple of grenades unnoticeably, let alone the .38 tucked into his trousers pocket. The trousers were also from Geary's, comfortably unconfining and made of a sturdy canvaslike material more suited to visiting farms than the ones that had irritated Sublette the day before.

"Installments make more sense for a farmer. He never knows when he'll need his cash for something," Brandon said. "I don't think Nonpareil's sold a windmill for cash on the spot except to the railroads, who want the cash discount, our president, Mr. Catesby, tells me. I certainly haven't made a full-price cash sale," he added, inwardly commenting: The truthful lie, Counselor, one of a trial lawyer's neatest tools; nice to find it still comes in handy.

"With those three, you better come with figures showing what it'll cost overall, and particularly how much they'll save by using the money they have instead of borrowing," Rattner said. "They're A-one loan prospects, but I'd rather lend it to the men that couldn't swing the windmills if I didn't, and there just isn't that much money to lend out. Now, this next bunch I'll lend to without even crossing my fingers; there's half a dozen of them, and at least two with the sense to see what a windmill could do for them. These two here, go for them before you try the others. If they take the mills, the rest are more likely to follow."

Brandon scanned the list and noted that Rattner had given rough traveling directions next to each name. The favored three at the top of the list all appeared to be close to town, which made sense; likely they were early comers and had first choice.

"The next some are the finger-crossers," Simon Rattner said. "Good, hard-working men, and none of them drawing bad luck like flies, which you'll sometimes see happening, but all more or less up against the wall, the way most farmers are nowadays. I'll have to look at their loans pretty carefully, and it could be I'd have to turn one or two down, but I'd try not to. I'd as soon not have to make the decision until we know better if the grasshoppers'll be back this year. If they come, all the windmills in Holland won't save a lot of those farms."

He slid another sheet of paper over to Brandon. "These are the ones I'd say you'd best pass by. Grasshoppers or not, they won't last long, and if they had the luck to scrape up a down payment, that's the last money you'd see, and I don't suppose it'd do Nonpareil to have title to an unpaid-for windmill rusting on an abandoned Nebraska farm."

"None at all," Brandon said, noting that the second list was short. "Nice to see there's so few of them."

"Few, but enough," Simon Rattner said gloomily. "Single men, all of 'em, and when they lose the farm they'll likely drift into town and add to the riffraff up at the north edge."

Brandon tucked the list into his pocket. "That where this Sublette fellow came from?"

Rattner nodded. "You remember what Swanson was saying yesterday about the fellows that got squeezed out of the cattle business coming on here. Like he said, there was farm work for some, but not most, and the ones left sort of squatted in the north edge of town, around the Seagull."

At Brandon's inquiring look Rattner went on. "A saloon and gambling place, only one in Bigsbee. Called that because of the seagulls that came and ate the hoppers back when the Mormons had their first harvest. Owner thought it'd be a good-luck name. Nice enough place until the drifters came in and sort of took it over. When Jere Sublette showed up some months back some of us figured he was the kind of man that could keep the drifters in line, which he sort of did, but it was his line, if you take my meaning. Thieving, some people out late held up, some beaten up for fun, and nothing much the police can do about it. You knocking him out yesterday, that'll make him bound and determined to get back at you, but it's also shown people he can be beat, and someday he'll be taken care of."

Came in from the west, could be Colorado, about the right time, Brandon thought. No reason he couldn't be this Farmer Dick or Neb I'm after, and he'd be one I wouldn't be any uneasy about killing. Could probably backshoot him with the whole town looking on and get elected mayor on the strength of it. Don't invest in that line too much, Counselor; all you're interested in is the genuine article, a man you'll know was with Gren Kenneally, and it don't do to get diverted by just anybody who'd be the better for a few ounces of lead in the face.

To Rattner he said, "Now I've got to start getting

around to bring the good word to all these folks. The livery stable at the west end of town the only place I can hire a horse and buggy?"

"Yeah," Rattner said. "Ed Marks's place. He knows horses, and the ones he hires out are trained and in good shape. He don't have any fancy buggies, but he's got a nice enough wagon, well sprung, with a hood that goes up over the seat."

"Good." A vehicle established a man as a serious sales representative, not just some fly-by-night riding through. Also, though Brandon had ridden hundreds of saddle miles—probably a thousand or more by now—he had never acquired the cowboy's devotion to life on horseback. He liked the idea of using a horse as a living locomotive, not as two extra pairs of legs under him.

"Marks is near enough the hotel so's you can stable the horse there," Simon Rattner said. "Hotel isn't geared to put guests' horses up, catering mainly to folks stopping over from the trains a day or so."

Brandon shook his head. "I won't be staying at the hotel. I got to thinking about it, and I saw I'd be better off boarding on a farm. I'd get to see what the local conditions are here, so I'd know better what the farmers need from a windmill and how the Nonpareil can work for them." In fact, Counselor, you'll get at least half an idea what a working farm is, so you won't make a total fool of yourself when you go around missionizing for Nonpareil. "Also, if I'm living on a farm, accepted by a farm family, I'm a little less a stranger, somebody to be suspicious of."

"Good idea," Simon Rattner said. "I'd say give Walter Kitson a try. He's over east. Got a fair piece of pretty good land his pa homesteaded, hard worker but short of money. He's on the crossed-fingers list for loans, but if he's got the sense to charge you Chicago prices for board, maybe he can afford to buy on installments."

"Trots along like Dan Patch, but's built stronger, can do light to medium loads without raising a sweat," Ed

Marks said, more in a spirit of frank admiration than in any attempt to promote his wares.

To Brandon the horse seemed both powerful and elegantly built, standing in its stall with an easy amiability suggesting that balking, kicking the dashboard to splinters, and bolting were not part of its repertory.

"Too good a horse by half for livery work, in fact," Ed Marks said. The stableman was a short, chunky man with a swarthy face, his appearance and his evident intimate feeling for horses reminding Brandon of some of the Gypsies who turned up at horse fairs outside St. Louis. "But he's just the thing for the work. Most livery places, they'll get some good-looking horses that could pass for a Thoroughbred with men that's seen engravings of such in the papers, that'll step high and look elegant pulling a surrey, and show a nice turn of speed on a paved road, but they'll founder if there's any real work called for. I paid too much for this one, but he's a dandy, ain't he?"

"Yah sure," Brandon said, realizing as he spoke that he had just seen the sun glint off Antonelli's sign down the street. "Uh, yeah, yes, he is."

Marks sighed. "You know what the farmers here need, Mr. Blake?"

"Windmills," Brandon said. "That's what they need, and that's what I'm here to sell them."

"Well, yes, I guess," Ed Marks said. "But before they worry about getting water to the crops they have to have the crops, and that means plowing and later on reaping. What the farmer needs is a good, powerful workhorse, and the folks around here just don't see it. They'll use oxen or any horse that's larger than a cow pony and think they've got a workhorse, and it just ain't, it's a joke. You ever been in St. Louis, Mr. Blake?"

Brandon suppressed a startled glance at Marks, who continued, "Or Milwaukee? Them big horses the breweries have, now, those are workhorses! Clydesdales and the like, or even Conestogas. A farmer that had himself a team or so of them, he'd get through his plowing in a quarter the time, like as if a steam engine was hauling the plow."

Brandon remembered seeing the giant horses pulling the Busch wagons to the city's *biergarten,* making the work seem effortless. Elise had said something funny about them . . . or was it Krista?

"If I could get some money together," Ed Marks said, "I'd get some workhorse stock, maybe Clydesdale, and start breeding. A few years, this corner of Nebraska'd be famous for 'em. But money's like quicksilver. You think you've got it in your hand, then it's gone and scattered."

"A lot of folks found that out in the Panic," Brandon said. "You want to show me how to hitch that horse up to the wagon?"

The track toward the Kitson farm led through lightly wooded low hills, and Brandon relaxed and let the horse find its way. What he was doing wasn't a bad idea for someone opening up a new territory for a line of goods meant to sell to farmers, and it hadn't been Ralph Catesby's idea, either. You put your mind to it, Counselor, he thought, and you wouldn't be a half-bad salesman. Not a bad life—see different parts of the country, different kinds of people, and you don't have to kowtow to any idiot who's got elected or appointed judge. The same could be said, he was disconcerted to realize a moment later, about his real occupation these days.

All the same, maybe he would have made a good salesman. He hadn't made a bad job of working as a reporter or gunman; not too convincing a gambler, but he had kept a bunch of men happily fed for the whole of a trail drive, which a lot of real cooks couldn't.

Was any of it as satisfying as the practice of law had been? Brandon rummaged in the recesses of his memory but could not summon up any sense of what it had been like. In fact, all of his life in St. Louis seemed to be distant. He could remember many scenes, but only in the static, one-color, remote fashion of photographs scanned in an album. The doings of Calvin Blake, Carter Bane, and the rest—the incidents of their occupations, their

travels, their confrontations with the men they hunted—
those were vivid and immediate.

Ned Norland's warning about not getting too involved
in the roles imposed on him—not wearing the mask too
tight—drifted back to him, and with a little effort he
dismissed it.

The road curved around a low hill and brought Brandon in sight of a farmstead, not large but well kept.
Something about what he saw produced an uneasy
stirring within him, a trailing touch of a cold finger. After
a moment he realized that the siting of the house and
barn in relationship to each other was very like Mound
Farm, and that he had often, approaching it, paused at
about this distance and taken in the view.

The fleeting perception of the resemblance passed. It
was in fact remote, since the Mound Farm house, once a
frontier trading post, was stone, and the barn was smaller
and different in style. In any case, this was clearly a
working farm, not a country home with a truck garden. A
fenced enclosure some distance from the main house
contained what looked like collapsed black or pink
balloons, which he identified after a moment as pigs.

The melons from Mound Farm had been particularly
sweet. . . . He could, it seemed to him, taste one now as
clearly as if he had just swallowed a cool morsel of the
flesh, and he was struck with a sudden pang of loss and
grief and remorse that left him weak and shaken, as if he
had survived a bolt of lightning.

"My aunt'll see to your washing, but it'll be extra,"
Walter Kitson said.

"That's agreeable," Brandon said, concealing his surprise and revising his impression of the household. The
woman who had met him at the farmhouse door had
introduced herself as Helen Kitson, and when he met
Walter Kitson a moment later he concluded that the
farmer had married a woman somewhat older than
himself. Brandon could easily see why he would; Helen
Kitson had a look of good-humored competence,

strength, and sensuality that suggested she would be a capable and comforting wife for a farmer, or pretty much any man.

Brandon found that he was slightly relieved to learn that she was Miss Helen, not Mrs. Walter. Kitson, though polite enough, seemed stiff and humorless, preoccupied with his farm, with a kind of cold self-absorption that could drain and age a wife without his ever being aware of it. Helen Kitson merited better than that, even though, keeping house for her nephew, she didn't seem to have found it yet. Her doing, presumably. Out here the languishing spinster lady overlooked by Cupid was unknown, with almost every nubile female either mated—singly or multiply, according to taste or trade—or determinedly discouraging suitors.

Walter Kitson had not charged Chicago prices for boarding Brandon, as Simon Rattner had wondered if he might, but he was not offering such a bargain as to make Brandon feel guilty—Omaha prices, maybe. But the neat, comfortable parlor and the appealing smells that drifted in from the kitchen were strong indications that the Kitson farm would be a good place to stay, and Helen Kitson had the demeanor of a first-rate hostess. She'd make a good manager for one of Jess Marvell's places, Brandon thought, and he found a curious pleasure in bringing the two women together in his mind.

"Board's breakfast and supper," Walter Kitson said. "You'll be away at your work daytimes, so's you won't be here for dinner, but she'll pack you a lunch basket if you want. That way you won't impose on the folks you're calling on."

"If you don't drop in at dinnertime expecting to be fed, they won't mistake you for a preacher, anyhow," Helen Kitson said.

"That ain't respectful, Helen," Walter Kitson said, with a perfunctory tone to the reproach that suggested he had given up some time ago on expecting his aunt to be respectful.

* * *

"You find lard works better?" Brandon said. "I've always used beef fat. Sears the meat fast, not much spattering."

"Our cows are dairy, not beef, so beef fat's not common here," Helen Kitson said, cutting a slab of meat into squares with a heavy-bladed knife. "We keep pigs, so lard is. You cook for fun, Mr. Blake?"

"Ah," Brandon said, realizing that chatting with Helen Kitson had led him to say more than he had meant to. "Well, I've done different kinds of jobs, and one was cooking." Forestalling any questions about what the different kinds of jobs were, he went on, "But this line I'm in now, that's first-rate work, I think. It's a wonder and a pride to see those windmills bringing up water to where it's needed, making farmland yield more." He patted the drawing laid out on the kitchen table, where he had been studying it and the book of instructions. So it is, Counselor, he told himself, and you didn't actually say you've sold any of those you've seen, did you?

"One of 'em would make a difference here come summer, sure enough," Helen Kitson said. "Even without the hoppers it's touch and go if the corn and wheat come to harvest or dry up. When my brother, Walter's dad, brought us out here, he told us what all the experts said: 'Rain follows the plow.' Once land starts being farmed, the rain comes along to make the crops grow. I can't imagine where they got such an outlandish idea or why sensible men were foolish enough to swallow it, but there it is. I think it's that if a man gets a notion in his head, he'll invent any kind of foolishness to dress it up, and my brother wanted to go west and farm, and so he made himself believe that trash." She poured a scoop of flour on the smooth board of the counter and began rolling the cut chunks of meat in it.

Ralph Catesby had told Brandon that the rain-follows-the-plow doctrine, seriously held by respected professionals, had probably created the biggest group of potential windmill customers by encouraging farming in unsuitable places. "It makes a great market for us,

Blake," he said, "but it also means we have to get to them fast. Otherwise, with folks of that cast of mind, somebody will come through selling gold bricks or machines guaranteed to print genuine U.S. currency and soak up all the available cash."

"He seems interested," Brandon said. "But I understand it's something he'll have to think over carefully."

"I never saw one of those things working," Helen Kitson said. "Is it like there's a chain of buckets going down into the well and the mill turning lifts 'em up and dumps 'em where they're wanted?"

"Not quite," Brandon said. He got up from the table and went to the sink, which boasted the uncommon luxury of its own pump. "There's a kind of rod that connects to the wheel up at the top, and when the wind spins it, the rod goes up and down and works a pump like this one, and there's your water."

Helen Kitson wiped her floured hands on her apron and came over to the sink. "That's a thing always touches me when I think about it, that pump. My brother didn't have to go to the bother. Most folks hereabouts just have the one in the yard. But I think he felt bad about bringing me out here, needed a woman to tend for him and Walter, with Pearl dead, and he did it to make up some. It does make it easier, almost like being in a house in a town."

"You've been out here a long time?" Brandon asked. Her hands, still dusted here and there with the flour, rested on the front of her checked cotton dress where it covered the swell of her thighs.

"Eight years," she said. "My brother came back from the War to find himself widowed, and he just couldn't settle into anything till he got the notion to come out here. He wore himself out getting the place going, then keeping it going in spite of the hoppers and bad times, and year before last he took pneumonia at the end of the winter and died. Walter's about keeping it afloat, which means he's doing better than some, but it's hard on him.

64

I do what I can to help, keeping house, doing chores, feeding him and the hands when we take 'em on for haying and harvest."

She was matter-of-fact about it, neither proud nor complaining. "Not an easy life for a woman," Brandon said.

Helen Kitson smiled, and Brandon was disturbingly aware of the change in the soft curve of her lips, then of the curves of her body under the faded dress. He looked at her with a quiet astonishment; she was a nice enough woman, good-looking, but the strength of his response to her was more than he would have expected.

"No, it isn't," she said. "But Mr. Blake, I don't know . . . do you know anyone you'd say has an easy life? Or anyone who's got a hard enough one that he'd really want to trade with anyone else? I don't think hard and easy are words you want to hang on life. Jobs are hard or easy, getting along with people is hard or easy, but living's what you do."

Brandon considered this silently. True enough, he thought. Whatever else I'd call my life lately, "hard" isn't the word. Crazy, maybe. And, yeah, Elise and the others dead, and me determined or doomed or whatever you call it to kill the men who did it, all that . . . and who would I trade lives with to get out of it? Ned Berns, that Ahrens took into the firm before I left, nice bright young fellow, nice pretty wife, nice neat house, nice neat future, everything a young man could want? Trade what I've been through and what's ahead for all those good things? No. Why *not*?

Helen Kitson moved to the sink, close to Brandon, worked the pump handle until water gushed from the spout, and washed the last of the flour off her hands, then dried them on her apron. "Sometimes what is hard is the wind," she said. "Blowing steady all the time, almost always from the northwest. You maybe don't notice it for a long time, then you do, and you realize it's been there all day so far, and it's going to be there the rest of the day and the next day. It gets so a big storm or a cyclone's a relief—at least it makes a change in where the wind's coming from. You know what I want, Mr. Blake?"

"What?" Brandon asked, speaking quickly so that he would not have time to think of what he might want Helen Kitson to want.

"An organ. Was a man came through selling them a year or so back. He had one that he carried in a wagon, not to everyplace he was calling on, but he got one lady in town to let him show it off in her house, and he told all the women he called on to come see it, and we mostly did. And it was wonderful. He worked the pedals till he could get air going through the pipes, and then he played us tunes. And I thought how wonderful it'd be to have music whenever I wanted it, and it's loud enough and fills the room so that you'd never have to hear the wind while it was playing."

She gave Brandon a smile, not resigned or rueful, just expressing pleasure at the thought of a room full of music, and said, "A good year, and the farm could clear enough to pay for a windmill and an organ, too. I'll hope so."

The picture Brandon had of her seated at the organ, legs rising and falling as she pumped the pedals, strong fingers moving surely across the keyboard, face tender and calm as she let the music flow from her center down the smooth arms and into the dancing fingers, was vivid and powerful. He looked at her, not much more than two feet away, and felt his own face lose tension, then became aware of the pulses on each side of his throat just under the angle of the jawbone.

Helen Kitson looked at him. Her smile faded, leaving her face thoughtful and grave for an instant, then returned. "I don't mind so much not having the organ, though," she said. "I'll tell you something I'd sooner you don't tell Walter, for he feels he's got to be my protector, being the man of the house, and there's times I think he thinks I'm his sister, and a younger one at that, instead of his aunt. But what I wanted to say, Mr. Blake, is that there's a gentleman in Bigsbee that . . . well, we have an understanding, you might say. Not an engagement. Walter would insist on us getting married if he knew, as that's the respectable thing, and I'd have to leave him to fend for himself, and he'd likely founder and be lost."

Whatever it was that was understood between Helen Kitson and her gentleman friend, she had gently made it clear that it excluded understanding anything about Calvin Blake beyond his roles as windmill salesman and boarder.

A little later, squatting in the henhouse and removing eggs from the nests, lifting the warm, soft-feathered birds when he had to and carefully placing the eggs in a large glazed bowl—a duty for which Helen Kitson had drafted him—Brandon supposed he was grateful that she had seen how strongly he was drawn to her and had rung down the curtain on whatever kind of drama there might have been.

A romantic entanglement, falling in love, with all its complications, would affect his mission disastrously and almost insure his failure to find any of the men he sought, or his death if he did find them.

On the other hand, a sordid physical liaison, with no emotional ties, though in many ways dangerous and certainly anathema to his old self, might not have been at all bad. It had been a long time, and Helen Kitson, without being pretty in the current fashion, was a strongly desirable woman.

He hefted a clucking chicken and said silently, Hey, Counselor, good story for you—ever hear the one about the traveling salesman and the farmer's *aunt?*

8

And you'll see, Mr. Swicegood, that the installments are set to come due not every month, but at the times of year when you could expect to be getting income from the farm. Nonpareil is aware of the problems of the farmer, and we make every effort to accommodate to his needs." Swicegood looked interested, but not avid, and Brandon was pretty sure he would not be opening his order pad on this visit. Farmers were methodical, doing things slowly. Men who moved suddenly and impulsively were likely to have bad experiences with the large animals and potentially lethal machinery they worked with.

"Well, it is a dandy-looking machine," the farmer said, looking again at the spread-out patent drawing. "And I *s'pose* it'll do what you claim."

"The Nonpareil is not magic," Brandon said, "but if you have a well with water in it, any model of the Nonpareil will draw up that water in quantities copious enough for stock feeding and crop irrigation beyond anything you have experienced so far."

"Hum," Swicegood said. "Lessee, income increases by a tenth, she'd have paid for herself not too much after the last installment's due. . . . Well, it sounds good, don't it? I'll consider it some and let you know. Leave a note for you at Edwards's when I've decided."

"I'll be passing this way in a few days and look in on you," said Brandon, who had no errands that would take him anywhere near the Swicegood farm, but who had already acquired the salesman's disinclination to let the customer call all the shots. "Thanks for your time, Mr. Swicegood."

He rolled up the drawing and gathered together the leaflets and papers demonstrating the Nonpareil line's amazing benefits, slid them into the carrying case, and picked up his hat. "Maybe you could help me with some information, sir. I mean to call on most of the farmers around here, and one I've got in mind is Mr. Harney, out a little other side of Bigsbee, toward the west. Would you say he'd be interested in learning about the Nonpareil windmills?"

Swicegood shook his head. "Interested, maybe, as there don't nothing interesting happen out there that I know of. A visit from a windmill salesman'd pass the time agreeable for him, I expect. But a customer he ain't. No money, and not likely to have any. One of them that come in from Colorado and Wyoming or the cow country in west Nebraska in the last year or so and homesteaded. Most of 'em didn't have the cash, real good land, or a wife, and you need all three to have a hope of makin' a go out here. Harney's place'll be on its way back to prairie this time next year, I'd bet."

This unpromising summary solidified Brandon's intention to visit Harney quite soon. To pass as a windmill salesman, he had to sell windmills, or to make creditable efforts at selling them, but he also had to pay attention to his real work, and Harney, however poor a prospect for Nonpareil's machines, could be the kind of man Brandon was hunting or be able to steer him toward that kind of man.

As Brandon turned to leave the farmhouse's front

room his eye was caught by a framed picture on the wall, a briskly rendered crayon drawing of a house—the one he was standing in, in fact. "Nice picture," he said.

"Yeah," Swicegood said. "Carl Swanson did it, didn't charge too much. He comes 'round to your place and talks you into it, and he either sits and draws it on the spot, or more likely he'll take a photograph and do the picture up back in town, frame it all nice like that, and bring it back and hang it where he thinks it should go."

"Clever fellow, Swanson," Brandon said. He left, turning over in his mind an idea that had suddenly sprung into it—there was a way Carl Swanson could be used to sweeten just a touch the prospects of selling Nonpareil windmills. And, no matter that it was a role he was acting, Brandon found he badly wanted to sell windmills.

"Are you sure you don't want to do this while I do that?" Helen Kitson called to Brandon.

Brandon grunted—not as loudly as the pig whose front legs he was doing his best to immobilize—as a sharp hoof took him in the shin. The thing about dealing with a pig was that you sort of had to get down to its level; and to grab it under whatever pigs had for armpits, you had to crouch and very likely, as he was doing now, wind up squatting or kneeling in the muddy, trampled farmyard. Helen Kitson seemed to be having an easier time of it, running a tape measure around the pig's chest, but Brandon suspected he would find it harder than what he was doing, which seemed to call only for brute strength and stubbornness, not skill or experience. "Better not. I never worked as a tailor," he said.

"Chest forty-four inches!" she called to Best, the Bigsbee butcher perched above them in his wagon who duly wrote on a sheet of paper next to him on the seat.

"Length forty-two!" Helen Kitson called.

"Um, forty-four times forty-four times forty-two . . . divide by four hundred . . . that's two hundred pounds, near enough," Best said.

"Two hundred three," Helen Kitson said. She draped the tape measure around her neck, picked up a bushel basket, and handed it to Brandon. "Put this over his head," she said.

As Brandon did so she bent over the pig's hindquarters, grabbed its tail with one hand, and pushed its flank with the other. The animal's squeals came through the basket amplified hollowly rather than muffled, but even as it protested it yielded and moved until its rear feet were at the foot of the plank ramp that led up to the wagon bed.

"Push!" Helen Kitson said. Brandon pushed on the pig's shoulders, holding the basket in place, and Helen Kitson pulled, twisting its tail and backing up the ramp; and the animal, squealing and scrabbling, slowly followed her. Flushed and disheveled, she looked, Brandon thought, splendid and even mythical, like the witch Circe dealing with one of Ulysses's men after she had turned them to swine.

Best took three more pigs, paid for them according to the weight Helen Kitson's measurements and the time-honored formula employing them indicated, and drove off.

"How accurate is that business with the tape measure and the multiplying and such?" Brandon asked. He sipped at a mug of coffee at the kitchen table while Helen Kitson re-counted the money Best had paid, then stowed it in a small chest.

"Near enough," Helen Kitson said. "Sometimes I guess the buyer gets a few pounds the best of it, sometimes the seller, so it works out, and no need to cart around big scales and try to wrestle the pig into them and keep him still while the weighing's done."

"I am all for anything that makes the process easier," Brandon said. He inspected his hands, considerably abraded from close contact with four bristly and determined pigs. "You know, when I saw his sign in town, Best Meats, I thought it meant that he sold prime meat, not his name."

"Well, it's the only meat store in town, so it's the best anyhow," Helen Kitson said. "Mr. Swanson wanted to make the sign read Best Quality Meats, so's it'd be taken both ways, but Best didn't want to pay but for the lettering for two words only."

Brandon recalled the trail drives he had seen passing, and the one he had been part of, and the whole rich, varied, high-spirited manner of life over much of the West that grew out of the cattle business; the larger-than-life figures of the cowboy, the rancher, even the rustler. He had not come out here to be part of it, but his mission had thrown him inevitably into it, even into employment by two ranchers. The epic drama of cattle ranching and its ritual last act, the trail drive, was never openly acknowledged by its actors, but it permeated their lives and made the grueling, tedious, often dangerous and poorly paid work an adventure that only crippling or death would make most of them abandon.

What prompted the recollection was the uneasy suspicion that what he and Helen Kitson had just done was not much different from what the imperious ranchers and the daring, dedicated cowhands did: getting meat animals away to where someone would kill them and sell the meat.

"You and Walter don't raise beef cattle?" Brandon said.

Helen Kitson shrugged. "About a third of what you feed a pig stays with it, turns into meat. Cattle, it's about a tenth. The only way beef cattle pay is if they feed themselves on free grass. If you pay for feed or have to raise it, pigs make sense and cows don't. And almost all of a pig is meat, and not much more than half a cow is."

"If pigs could be raised that way," Brandon said lightly, "there might be big pig ranches and pig trail drives."

"Huh," Helen Kitson said, and she thought about this for a few seconds. "I doubt you'd get many men longing for the wild, free life of a pigboy!"

She was still chuckling at the thought, and Brandon grinning, when the door from the yard opened and Walter Kitson stepped into the kitchen.

He gave them both a squinting look. Brandon wondered if he thought they might be sharing some improper secret, then decided that Walter Kitson probably distrusted laughter on general principles.

"Passed Best on the road as I was coming from Bigsbee," he said. "I thought I'd be back earlier, in time to get the hogs loaded, but—"

"But, like you saw," Helen Kitson said, "I got 'em weighed and loaded very nicely, with Mr. Blake helping. He didn't know anything about it, but he learns fast."

"I don't know if you learned it fast or already knew it," Walter Kitson said, "but you seem to have handled that Sublette darned well. I just heard about it from some of the men at Edwards's store; you didn't say anything about it when you came here."

"Didn't occur to me," Brandon said. "Or maybe I thought you might not want a brawler for a boarder."

"Any man that can brawl with Sublette and win is welcome here, boarder or not," Walter Kitson said. "That man is living proof that Satan walks among us and his servants are legion. The lowlifes and bummers that hang around the Seagull were bad enough as they were, but since he's come they're a menace. The police can't do anything, and I don't know how long it can go on this way."

He looked at Brandon. "If you were in a business here, Mr. Blake, a permanent resident, you could probably be an important man. You knew how to stand up to Sublette, and what's more, you had the nerve to do it, and that hasn't been seen here in some time, maybe never. I'm not ashamed to say that I couldn't do it, for nobody else could, either."

"But I'm transient," Brandon said. "Sell what windmills I can, see them put up and working, and I'm on the next train out."

"Funny you should say that," Walter Kitson said. "You know what I think about Sublette coming in and taking charge of the riffraff?"

"That you don't like it?" Brandon said. Helen Kitson, in his line of sight but not her brother's, rolled her eyes and pantomimed a yawn.

"Well, that, of course," Walter Kitson said. "But I have figured out what's behind it all."

"Behind it?" Brandon said.

"The railroad!" Walter Kitson said. "They are squeezing us to death with freight rates, and they have settled this army of thugs amongst us in case we get any ideas of doing anything about it! Somebody was seen nosing around the Grange building some nights ago, and they chased him away, but it shows you—the Grange is fighting the railroads, and now look what happens."

Brandon thought that Walter Kitson had a lot of learning to do. There was no need to postulate sinister plans behind unpleasant happenings; the ordinary run of shiftlessness and malice encountered almost everywhere could produce any amount and variety of bad results. On the other hand, Jere Sublette and John B. Parker seemed to have something in common: the habit of walking over—or even through—people to get what they happened to want at the moment.

Harney's farm looked as if it could serve as an illustration in one of the weeklies for the effects of the depression: "Scene of Desolation on the Battlefield Between Hope and the Forces of Nature and Economics, Engraved from Life." A small boxy building constructed of slabs of sod and roofed with turf, inappropriately cheerful with fresh grasses and small red wildflowers, was recognizable as the farmhouse only because there seemed no other function for it. A larger structure, of warped planks of weathered wood, could be either a large shed or small barn. Beyond them Brandon could see plowed furrows with a light fuzz of green coating them; the cultivated area didn't seem large enough to produce enough of whatever it was to keep Harney solvent.

A bony horse stood patiently, reins dropped over a fence rail in the yard between the house and the barn. It nosed at the muddy yard as if, in spite of all the evidence, there might be a blade or so of grass to chew on if it searched hard enough.

Brandon dismounted from the wagon and tethered his horse to the same railing. The other animal looked sweaty and was breathing heavily. Ridden recently, and not very carefully. That suggested a visitor; Harney's horses would be stabled in the barn.

He walked toward the sagging building, seeing strips of daylight through the upper portion and noting that it leaned perceptibly toward the southeast; the prevailing wind would collapse it like a folded pasteboard box if it wasn't shored up pretty soon. The squat cylinder of a section of log stood by the near corner with a hatchet stuck into it and a crudely shaped length of raw wood leaning against it. Brandon supposed that Harney had started making something he needed around the farm and stopped that in favor of doing something else; the look of the farm suggested that kind of farmer.

He heard some indistinguishable, but by the tone unfriendly, words in a grating voice as he approached the barn's entrance. A visitor, all right, unless Harney was in the habit of scolding himself. "Hello the barn!" he called.

The voice stopped. Brandon rounded the corner of the barn and saw the doorway, with the door leaning at an angle suggesting that it was a long time since it had been slid shut. Inside, a skinny man in shabby work clothes, with a discouraged stoop and a seamed face that added a decade to his actual age—probably late twenties, Brandon thought—looked at him inquiringly, past the man he had been talking to, or listening to.

This man was turning to look toward the doorway as Brandon came into it, and he gave a snarl of recognition. "Goddamn tricksy dude! No man don't use Jere Sublette so an' keep his parts an' particklers! Perpare to eat yer own balls after as I rip 'em off, dude, for you don't git to try the same monkey tricks on me twicet!"

Brandon agreed with Sublette's estimate of the usefulness of his previous tactics and had stepped back to the chopping block and retrieved the hatchet before Sublette had finished speaking.

9

Sublette started toward the doorway, but he halted when Brandon hefted the hatchet and cocked his arm for a downward chop or a throw.

"Jist th'ow it an' I'll dodge an' come at you an' twist yer haid off," Sublette said.

"Maybe," Brandon said. "And maybe it'll move faster than you do. Or maybe I'll hang onto it and amputate a hand or so when you come at me. Try it."

"I might just will," Sublette said, flexing his knees as if preparing for a spring at Brandon.

"Don't," Harney said. Brandon saw that he had got hold of a pitchfork and was pressing the tines lightly against Sublette's back.

"Hey, Art," Sublette protested, "you don't want to go interferin' in my business with this dude, an' you wouldn't dast use that anyways."

"I as soon done it before," Harney said, "but it would have meant law trouble, and you ain't worth it. Now I got a witness and I got cause, so if you don't want your tripes ventilated, git on out of here, Jere." He gestured toward the doorway with the pitchfork.

Brandon stepped to one side as Sublette approached,

and he kept the hatchet held ready for action. It was like being in the forest as an old, massive bear shambled by—the rumbling growl, the fetid smell, the red-eyed glare. At the doorway he turned and said, "You gotta lay down that fork sometime, Art, an' that hatchet ain't grafted to yer hand, dude. Make up yer minds to it, yer hides is already pegged out an' dryin'. Only thing needs settled is when. Think on it, gents."

Brandon and Harney watched as Sublette mounted his horse and rode off. "You met Jere before, huh?" Harney asked.

Brandon explained their encounter, and Harney said, "Wisht I'd been there to see it. Jere'd take that hard, I can see. He don't like to look foolish."

"He won't like what happened just now any better," Brandon said.

"Yeah," Harney said. "Maybe I'd best have run him through and let you back me up to the cops that I had to. He'll have it in for me, but, tell you the truth, I don't much care."

He gestured at the house, the cultivated land, and the barn. "I'm plugging away at this until I know all the way down that it's no good, but I'm getting there, and likely I won't be around much longer. Might not be so bad if Jere did try something. It'd make up my mind to pull out."

Harney looked at Brandon. "Anyhow, you come out here for something, and I expect it wasn't for a run-in with some crazy man."

Well, it is, Brandon thought, if you accept that anyone who'd do what Gren Kenneally's men did at Mound Farm has to be crazy.

"Well, it almost makes me feel like a real live farmer again to have somebody trying to sell me something, Blake," Harney said after Brandon had extolled the Nonpareil line's virtues. "But you've seen the place, and even if you was giving the windmills away, I doubt it would do much good here. If what I got planted grows, I ain't got the damn machines to harvest it beyond a rusted-out old reaper that'll likely fly apart when I try to use it."

"Haven't had the best of luck, I see," Brandon said. "You been here long? Come from Ohio or someplace?"

"Two years and some," Harney said—if truthfully, removing himself from consideration as possibly being the man in Jess Marvell's report, whose stated intention to go from Colorado to Nebraska dated from no more than four months ago. "Used to be a cowhand out in Montana and Wyoming, but it come on hard times in the cattle trade there, and I come on this way. Took the notion to be a farmer and homesteaded this land, but I guess I ain't cut out for it."

Cut out or not, he didn't have the prime land, the cash stake, and the woman, the three requisites for success Swicegood had mentioned. "Did you know Sublette before? I heard he came here from that way."

Harney nodded. "He wasn't so bad out there, or maybe it's just that there's more wildness in cow country, and he didn't stand out like he does here. But when he turned up here he wanted me to be part of the crowd he's gathered around him at that saloon in town, go in with him on schemes he's planned, and I wouldn't."

"Indeed," Brandon said politely.

Harney grinned wryly. "Yeah, he had a reason to hope I'd throw in with him, or thought he did. Cowboying don't pay much above nothing even when there's enough work, and the wages somehow don't stay with a man, so I took to doing some wide-looping now and again. Built up a little stake from it, which is how I could afford this miserable heap of crap here. Jere done some rustling himself and knowed about me, so when he come here he looked me up, said he'd spread the word about what I done if I didn't jine up with him."

"Didn't worry you," Brandon said.

"I think being bad-mouthed by Jere Sublette would be as good as a handshake from the mayor, once you git to know Jere," Harney said. "Also, farmers don't think much of cattlemen anyhow and ain't about to get excited over someone who's lightened some rancher's pockets a little."

He looked over his property and sighed. "You ain't got two pins about you anywheres, have you, Blake? If you did, and cared to hand 'em over, I as soon borrow the loan of a match from you, too, and set the barn alight and turn the animals out to find their own food and move on."

"No pins," Brandon said.

"Then I'll stick it out a while longer," Harney said. "How long a while I can't say. Maybe till I get word the Fool Killer's been sighted nearby, and I'd best get away before he comes for me."

The north edge of Bigsbee bore out its reputation as Brandon drove through it on his way from Harney's farm. It was a sprawl of small frame houses and outright shacks, dispirited and dusty, looking like the fringes of a railroad cow town more than the outskirts of a prospering—once-prospering, anyhow—farming community. It was here that the displaced cowhands and such had drifted and fetched up, like tumbleweeds ranged against a stand of cactus. A few streets or alleys or paths—it was hard to know what to call the open spaces between the huddles of buildings—over, the two stories of the Seagull towered above the saloon's surroundings. As Brandon's wagon passed he saw here and there a furtive face peering around a building corner, and sometimes the back of a figure hurrying toward the Seagull. It looked as though the passage of a vehicle was enough of a novelty here to rate immediate reporting to Jere Sublette, doubtless brooding in his headquarters.

Brandon eased the .38 from his pocket and laid it on his lap. An attack here was unlikely, and being ready for the unlikely was an excellent way to stay alive.

He looked over toward the saloon and the white-painted wood effigy of a flying bird hanging in front of it. The wing tips showed fingerlike separate feathers, not single points, suggesting that the bird had been carved by someone more used to eagles than seagulls, or who had just perhaps misheard the order. Jere Sublette seemed less and less likely to be the man he sought here. For one thing, "Farmer" anything was an improbable name for anyone to have called him. "Killer," "Cyclone," "Cowpat," all of those fit some aspect of his nature, but not "Farmer."

All the same, this was the likeliest place for his man to be, where most of the men who came here to make a living farming wound up. The north edge was where he would have to find a way to hunt, and that meant dealing, one way or another, with Jere Sublette.

There was almost no transition between the north edge and the solid, respectable portion of Bigsbee; one side of a street was shantytown, the other well-kept houses, with, Brandon noticed, substantial, high, gateless fences around their backyards. The effect was something like fortified trading posts he had seen in country where Indians were a danger.

Now to do something about the idea that had come to him a couple of days back in Swicegood's front room. . . . In a minute or so he turned left on Main Street and stopped the horse in front of Carl Swanson's shop.

The clank of the bell as he opened the door summoned Swanson from a room behind the counter.

"Oh, yeah," the sign painter-photographer said, "Mr. Blake. What can I do for you? Want me to do a sign to hang on that surrey, a nice painting of one of your windmills? Company name and all, make it look like it was your own rig instead of hired."

"Other way around," Brandon said. "I understand you do pictures of folks' farmhouses for them. What about painting a picture of the owner's house, or whatever else he wants, along with the name, on the windmill itself? There's plenty of room on the wind vane, and it'd look mighty pretty if you used bright colors, shining in the sun. I think if I could offer that, it'd make the deal look sweeter. Any idea what it'd cost?"

"Not much," Swanson said. "So long's you could bring the whatsit, the vane, in here to work on. I am not no Michelangelo, to go climbing up a ladder to do my painting." He thought a moment and said, "Now, that is some idea, using that surface like that. But there might be a better one. Say I was to do a picture and notice for stuff like Hop Bitters or Hamlin's Wizard Oil or Williams's Pink Pills for Pale People or Kickapoo Indian Sagwa, Nature's Own Remedy, respectable medicines like that? I have done some of those for barns and sheds and one on a nice chalk bluff that the railroad passes by, and the agents for those companies pay nicely for the use of the space, as well as for the painting. I don't know what the rate would be for a windmill vane, but it'd be something, and I expect the farmers I know would rather have a little extra cash than the glory of seeing their house and name up on a windmill."

Brandon abandoned his own inspiration without regret. Starting up the sales talk with the offer of a chance to make money would get things going briskly. "I'd be grateful if you could find out what they'd pay," he said.

"I'll put a letter on the afternoon train to Omaha," Swanson promised. He looked past Brandon as the bell on the door announced the entry of another customer. "Afternoon, Mr. Kitson, here's Mr. Blake, too."

"In the market for a windmill, are you, Swanson?" Walter Kitson said, nodding to Brandon.

"He may be able to help me sell them," Brandon said, and he explained the idea of selling advertising space on the vane.

"That'd help," Walter Kitson said. "Pay by the month for as long's the advertisement's up, don't they, Swanson?"

"Some do. Some pay by the quarter. Now, you'll be here for the picture of your pa, is that it?"

"Helen said it should be ready by now."

"Miss Helen's right, it is." Carl Swanson disappeared into the back room.

"We had an old photograph of my father," Walter Kitson said to Brandon. "Tintype, with a big crease across it, and kind of spotted. Helen took the notion to have Swanson take it and make a crayon drawing of it and put a frame around it. She thinks he does good work and wanted a nice picture of Pa. I don't see the sense of it, but she's his sister, and she wanted it, and she's paying for it with her egg money, so it's no bother to me. Now, if I worked it out so's I could buy one of your windmills, I wouldn't want advertisements for liquor or tobacco on it. Those medicines, they're respectable and useful, but I don't hold with promoting smoking and strong drink."

Lunsford Ahrens & Brandon had a small but steady clientele of patent medicine manufacturers who sometimes needed court representation, and Brandon knew that most of the nostrums approached cheap whiskey in their alcohol content, to say nothing of the generous splash of opium some of them employed.

"Here it is," Carl Swanson said, displaying a meticulously executed crayon portrait of a broad-faced man with abundant side whiskers and a placid smile. Brandon could see a faint trace of Helen Kitson in the features.

"A lot happier-looking than I remember him, or than the photograph was," Walter Kitson said, looking at the portrait with some suspicion.

"Miss Helen asked me to do him a little less severe than the photo showed," Carl Swanson said. "Very thoughtful lady, Miss Helen." It seemed to Brandon that he took pleasure in saying her name. He wrapped the picture in brown paper and handed it to Walter Kitson.

Another ring of the bell ushered Geary, the clothier and haberdasher, into the shop.

"Blake, Kitson, good to find you both here," he said. "You, too, Swanson, but I'd expect that, wouldn't I? I was just up at Edwards's store, and there was word that Jere Sublette's boiling mad about something, and everybody's afraid of what'll happen. Rumor that it had to do with you, Blake, anything in that?"

"I ran into him while I was with a customer," Brandon said. "We had some words and he went off, no blows struck."

"I wish there had been!" Walter Kitson said. "On Sublette, anyhow. That man's an abomination!" Brandon wondered what Kitson would do if he found himself face to face with Sublette and holding a hatchet. He considered it a six-to-four chance that Kitson would try to use it, and much shorter odds that Sublette would take it away from him and make him eat it.

"I don't know how long we're supposed to take it!" Geary said. He and Walter Kitson indulged in a duet of railing against Jere Sublette and his satellites for a few minutes, seeming to take Swanson's and Brandon's agreement for granted. Geary's concern seemed to be mainly with property damage and challenge to the foundations of social order; Kitson stuck to drunkenness, gambling, and, in particular, fornication.

Brandon glanced at Carl Swanson, who looked troubled. The atmosphere Kitson and Geary had churned up in the store seemed to Brandon like that just before a storm, still but ominous, charged with electricity; the two angry men were like dust devils, the miniature cyclones that spring up and skitter across the earth before the storm breaks.

Walter Kitson and Geary left, and Brandon said, "What's your notions about Sublette?"

Carl Swanson shrugged. "An abomination, like Walter says, but that's not much out of the ordinary these days. He has hurt people, and it'd be better if there was a way to stop him, but there's other things to worry about. Paying too much attention is one thing that gives him a lot of power. I think you've done it right. You don't know he's alive till he gets in your way, then you boot him out of it. Seems to me that's what you've done so far. Everybody else did that, he wouldn't last long."

"That was nice work you did on Walter's pa," Brandon said.

"Miss Helen wanted a good picture, and I tried to

make it look like a face you'd want to have looking at you all the time. Most people, that ain't easy," Carl Swanson said. "But I think I did it, and I know it's a good drawing."

"Different from signs and advertisements," Brandon said.

Carl Swanson shrugged. "They're what's wanted, and they make my living for me. It ain't easy sometimes to keep in mind that I can do good work while I'm doing a patent medicine puff on a barn or a rock, or making somebody's rickety farmhouse look like a mansion. But it's how I keep going and sometimes find the time to do the work I'm good at." He looked at Brandon. "Your work takes you around the West considerable, I expect?"

"I've been across a good deal of it," Brandon said.

"So've I," Carl Swanson said. "All around, photographer and sign painter. And I took photographs all over the place, mountains, desert, towns, prairie, cows, cowboys, saloons, whorehouses. It's easier nowadays, 'cause you can make up plates ahead of time and don't have to have a darkroom wherever you go; you can take pictures anywhere you can lug a camera. I took 'em mainly 'cause I thought I'd do a whole galleryful of paintings, and I wanted the photos as first sketches that I could copy back in the studio. But I got more interested in the photographs themselves, for there's something about 'em that even the most elegant crayon drawing or oil painting don't have. There's a whole photography building at the Exposition, and I'd admire to get to see it, but I don't expect I'll get there. Anyhow, when you've got some time I'd be interested to know what you think of my photos. Miss Helen Kitson thought they were pretty good."

"I'll come by and have a look when I can," Brandon said.

"Well, I will, then," Swicegood said. "I was still turning it over in my mind, but since you come by here, and there is the extra of the income from the advertising, why, I'll go for it! I'll want the Kickapoo Sagwa, for it's eased my aches and let me get on with the work many's the time. If they pay as well as the others, that is."

"I believe the rates are pretty much standard," said Brandon, who had not heard from Carl Swanson and had no idea whatever of the payment practices of billboard, barn, and now windmill advertisers.

"Delivery within ten days, you said?" Swicegood asked.

"From receipt of the order, which will be wired to Chicago first thing in the morning," Brandon said. With a stirring of excitement he slipped the elastic band from around his order pad, pulled out three copies of the form—one for the office, one for him, one for the customer, and they had better be made out identically to the letter—set them on Swicegood's writing table, and began to write up the order that deprived the pad of its virginity and breathed reality into Calvin Blake, salesman.

10

The morning air was cool, close to chilly, and Brandon was grateful for the warmth that spread out from the iron kettle and the brisk fire under it. Helen Kitson's face was flushed and moist as she stood over the kettle, obliged to be closer to the fire than was comfortable by the need to stir the melting fat.

A quarter mile to the east Brandon could see the tiny figure of Walter Kitson riding the horse-drawn cultivator, which looked like a nightmarish, many-legged predatory insect clawing its way across the earth. Not totally easy work, he thought, but less demanding than what his aunt was doing right now.

"All melted now," Helen Kitson said. She sniffed the steam above the kettle. "Tallow'd make for harder soap, but pork fat does fine. Can you fetch me that crock over here?"

Brandon took the stone crock and, at her direction, held it up over the kettle at one side. She took the lid off, set it on the ground, and took hold of the crock's bottom. "You just hold it steady over the kettle, and I'll tilt."

Brandon's eyes watered as the lye poured from the crock into the hot fat, and he realized why soap-making had to be done out of doors. He held his breath until Helen Kitson let the crock return to an upright position and clapped the lid on again.

"If you'll just stir, I'll go get the molds," she said. Brandon took the long-handled wooden paddle and moved it around in the pungent liquid in the kettle. The fumes stung his eyes, and the side of one hand burned where a little lye had spilled on it from the crock. He rubbed the hand on his trousers, with no noticeable effect. His shoes were absorbing heat from the fire and acting on his feet much as bread pans do on baking loaves; but he could not move back much and still keep stirring.

I guess this is one of those gentle domestic tasks suited to the dainty fingers and delicate natures of the female sex the ladies' magazines talk about, Brandon thought. He had seen *Macbeth* once and felt like one of the witches at the cauldron. What was in there was rougher stuff than eye of newt or toe of frog, though.

Helen Kitson returned with three long rectangular tubs of wood, which she set on the ground. "The molds," she said. "My father made them back home a long time ago. The soap sets up in long bars, and you cut it up in cakes later on. I wish there were different shapes, like an egg or an apple or something. But I guess soap, you wash yourself with it, and you wash your clothes, and that's it. Doesn't matter what shape it is."

She took the paddle from him and took over the stirring with a steady, rhythmic ease of motion.

"This seems like pretty hard work for a woman," Brandon said.

"Harder than some work, easier than some," Helen Kitson said. "Dusting, that's easier. Pig killing, that's harder. Most work is hard, women's or not. I expect that's why they call it work. Hard isn't the worst of it; if you can do it, you get used to it, if you live. There's more farm widowers than farm widows. But I'll tell you, Mr. Blake, what is wearisome more than I can say is that it's the same work over and over. You dust and sweep, and tomorrow it's to do over. Cook dinner today, cook dinner again tomorrow. Make soap, it gets used up, you make soap again. It's . . ." She stirred the paddle with extra force, and some blobs of the fat-lye mixture splashed out of the kettle.

"It's that nothing's ever *done,*" she said after a moment. "I know, a lot of men's work is like that, too, but almost *all* a woman's work is. If you build a house or a railroad, well, it's there, and you go on to the next thing. You sell a windmill, and up it goes, and the farmer's got water he didn't have. You made a change in things. Women just keep things going in the same place, like the wheel on those windmills."

Brandon found that keeping things going in the same place was what he had always expected women to do—tending families, supporting their men so they could go out and do . . . well, real work. Work that changed things, if you wanted to look at it that way.

Now, why ever do you think that, Counselor? he asked himself. There's Krista, running the Ostermann businesses, and Jess Marvell—she's making big changes, for sure. That notion of women's work, is that something got into your head when you were a pup, and you never bothered to look at it since?

"There's to be a women's pavilion at the Centennial," Helen Kitson said. "Women's inventions, women's businesses, women's painting and statues. That would be something to see. I can't go, but I hope lots of women do and go home fired up to see what they can do."

Brandon wondered if the man she had an "understanding" with in Bigsbee looked on her as a revolving wheel, going through the daily round but always starting each day from the same place she had started the last.

"This batch won't be hard for a week or so," Helen Kitson said, "but there's some left from the last making. Will you want a bath Saturday? I'm heating water for Walter, and it wouldn't be that much extra trouble."

Brandon had been sponging himself sketchily at the kitchen pump in the mornings and considered that he was due for a bath at least by Saturday; but the conversation with Helen Kitson made it impossible to overlook that she would be heating a wash boiler full of water on the stove, then lugging it to wherever the tub was, then emptying the tub, a respectable job of work for a stevedore.

Of course, he could help, but . . . A vivid picture formed in his mind of Helen Kitson pouring water over his naked body as he sat, or stood, in the tin tub. It was followed immediately by the mental image of him pouring water over her, which he had considerable difficulty in dismissing.

"Ah, thank you," he said. "I'm going into town to see if there's a confirming wire from Chicago about Swicegood's order, and while I'm there I'll get a shave and a bath at the barbershop."

Also, his hand still stung from the lye, and the prospect of lathering himself all over with the fume-emitting substance that Helen Kitson was stirring did not appeal strongly to him.

ORDER BEING CRATED STOP WILL SHIP VIA RAIL WHEN DRAFT CLEARS STOP CATESBY

"No 'Well done, pass out cigars and nuts,' huh?" the telegraph office clerk and operator said as Brandon read the telegram.

"Very businesslike, my boss," Brandon said. "Knows my work, expects me to sell, doesn't see any need to carry on about it." Privately he considered that the telegraphic equivalent of setting off fireworks would have been appropriate to the circumstances; he'd worked and thought hard for that sale, and it deserved to be recognized.

"It's a wonder how fast things get done nowadays," the clerk said. "I hit the key here, and in less time than you can measure it's clicking in Omaha or Chicago or New York, and then there's fast trains carrying us and anything we want from the Atlantic to the Pacific in less time than it took those old Mormons to push their handcarts from one water hole to the next. And next there'll be balloons with engines flying crost the country, and an operator in Ohio I talk to sometimes when the line's quiet, he tells me there's a kind of telegraph just patented that'll carry voices."

"There is always talk like that," Brandon said. "Machines that fly, wires that talk, perpetual motion engines. Real inventions, steamboats and the telegraph and windmills and such, they're straightforward, not outlandish."

"If you was to see what they'll have in Philadelphia, you'd maybe think different," the clerk said. "Wonders of industry and artifice from the world over assembled in the Hall of Mechanics for all to marvel at. Folks lucky enough to go there, they'll be seeing the world of tomorrow."

As Brandon left the office he considered the idea of a world of tomorrow and found it uninspiring. Haven't even made the world of today work yet, he thought.

At Geary's store he found the haberdasher expressing something of the same thought: The chief impediment to the perfection of today's world was Jere Sublette, well ahead of grasping railroad magnates and grasshoppers.

Instead of replying to Brandon's request for half a dozen pair of socks, he leaned over the counter and said, "There was a fire there last night!"

"Three black, three brown," Brandon said.

"In the north edge!"

"I think wool, but maybe you've got some cotton you could let me look at."

"You know what that means?" Geary said hoarsely.

That it is easier to get a telegram to San Francisco than an order for socks into your head, Brandon said sourly and silently. Maybe that talking telegraph, if there was any such thing, might get your attention. Only way to the socks is to follow you through whatever territory your mind's stampeding in and try to head you back to business. "Some drunk got careless with matches?"

"Maybe, maybe not. I think they're practicing."

Geary took Brandon's bemused pause for an expression of interested inquiry and said excitedly, "Remember the Chicago Fire? When the whole downtown started to burn the loafers and the gamblers and the whores and the crooks, they went through and looted everything from stores, homes, wherever. The biggest robbery in the history of the country, storefuls of stuff stolen, jewels, silk, furniture, money, whatever there was. Well, by God, Blake, I think that's what Sublette's planning. When the wind and weather's right, first dry spell we get, he's gonna fire those shacks in the north edge, and they'll catch like tinder, and the fire and sparks'll set the rest of Bigsbee on fire, and she'll burn all the way to the river, just like it happened in Chicago. And Sublette and his crowd, they'll do what the scum in Chicago did, spread out, robbing and murdering. It's bound to come to that."

Geary stared intently at Brandon; his hands, spread on the counter, flexed as if trying to crawl away, spiderlike, on the spread fingers.

It's growing in him, Brandon thought. Hipped on it the other day with Walter, but worse now. Sublette's bad medicine, all right, but he's got this one spooked past reason. "Ah, how did you come to work the, uh, whole idea out?"

"It's the only thing that makes sense," Geary said. "There is some good cotton lisle with double woven bottoms that should do you nicely."

At Edwards's store Brandon was pleased to find himself hailed, after only a few days in town, as a regular member of the informal group around the coffeepot in the back room. His sale to Swicegood, published to the town at large by the telegraph clerk, who seemed to have little patience with the idea of confidentiality, came in for congratulation and an expression of hope that it might be a small omen of better times—an improvement in anybody's fortunes might affect those of the rest of Bigsbee, however slightly.

"And what's this I hear about you taking on Sublette in

a duel with double-bitted axes?" Carl Swanson said. "If you'd told me about it ahead of time, I'd have come along and sketched it for the Omaha or Chicago papers."

"Got his ear with you?" Edwards said. "I heard you sliced it off before you hit him on the head with the flat of the ax and knocked him out."

"As you damn well know," Brandon said, "that account got blown up on the way here like a balloon at a state fair. That's one reason hearsay's no good as testimony. What you hear gets distorted by the time you say it. As a lawyer I met told me," he added hastily, cursing the relaxed atmosphere that had allowed Cole Brandon to emerge and make a comment Calvin Blake would not have made.

He explained what had happened, which the other men found at least as interesting as the fable that had reached them, and said, "If Geary'd heard that story, he'd probably have given me these socks free." Geary's theory about Sublette's incendiary plans was news to them, and when he had finished recounting it they looked troubled.

"Saul's not a bad fellow, or crazy," Edwards said after a minute. "But he's going through bad times. Maybe no worse for him than for the rest of us, but he feels it. He don't like to think it's just bad luck, or even maybe something he might be able to do something about. For him it needs to be that there's somebody doing it to him. He's like folks that can't get anything out of religion unless there's Satan to fight."

"Need the devil as much as they need God, to make sense out of things," Carl Swanson said. "Maybe more."

"Though with John B. Parker and them going up and down in the earth and seeking whom they may devour," Edwards said, "a man might be forgiven for thinking that there's devils around, if not Old Scratch himself. If the bastard railroads kill off farming with the high rates, they'll be killing themselves, too, so it don't make sense."

"You know," one of the other men said, "there are going to be all kinds of new railroad cars showed at the

Exposition, and there is going to be a kind of car that sits on top of a rail and runs all over the fairgrounds."

The mood in Edwards's back room lightened with the excuse to drop the consideration of hard times and the remote possibility of an arsonist invasion from the north end in favor of dwelling on the endless delights of the Centennial Exposition.

"It's sort of foolish," Edwards muttered to Brandon, "but it kind of takes us out of ourselves for a while. You know, there's men here that're still sore at some of the others because of which side they fought on in the War, but you get 'em on the Exposition and Rebel or Federal don't matter anymore, so it's worth a little foolishness."

"There's to be a photographers' hall there," Carl Swanson said dreamily. "Work from all over the world, England, Japan, and pictures from all the top photographers here, Sarony, Brady, Broadbent. Portraits of beautiful women from Austria-Hungary, beggars from Japan, landscapes of the West. Damn, but I'd like to see it! And even worse, I'd like to have had a chance to get my pictures shown there. I'd stack 'em up against any I've seen."

"They are good, Carl," a man said. "Some of them mountain pictures you took, a man could about get dizzy and fall off."

"If you got a few minutes, we could go over and I could show 'em to you," Swanson said, turning to Brandon.

Brandon had had few dealings with photographers, but he knew enough about enthusiasts to be sure that Swanson's few minutes would be closer to an hour. But once he had completed his errands there were no urgent calls on his time. "I've got to do a few things, but I'll come by your place when they're done."

11

Nothing wrong with the axle, that wobble's just the wheel a little loose at the hub. I'll have it on tight in an hour and check the others. She'll ride smooth again when you leave, don't doubt it."

"Good enough," Brandon said.

Ed Marks looked at the wagon. "That is a pretty good buggy, and I keep it in good shape. But I would surely like to see what they'll have at the Exposition—there is a whole big building, hundreds of feet on a side, to show wagons and carriages from all over the world. And then there'll be the best horses from everywhere, too, and the newest kind of binders and reapers and everything else! I tell you, Mr. Blake, it'd be like a drunk getting the key to a grog shop for me to go there."

"You told me how you feel about workhorses," Brandon said, "and you rent out carriages, so I can see you'd want to see what new kinds there are. But how come you'd be interested in reapers and such?"

"I've been thinking about it," Ed Marks said. "With the horses, if I had the kind I want—the Clydesdales and even heavier—if I had those and I had the reapers and binders as well, why, I could hire out to do the work. The newest machines, and enough strong horses to pull them, I'd get through the work in a quarter the time most of 'em take now, go from farm to farm. It'd bring farming into the twentieth century before we're shut of the nineteenth."

"I read that they're trying steam engines to pull farm machinery, some places," Brandon said.

Ed Marks spat on the ground. "A steam engine's no good for farm work. You need animals that've been bred to it, handled by men that know it. And a steam engine don't manure the ground while it's working it. Stinking, worthless teakettles, that's what steam engines are."

"Couldn't have trains without them," Brandon said.

"Trains are trouble," Ed Marks said. "If there was no trains, things'd be a lot better. You don't need to get anyplace faster than a good horse and rig will take you."

Given the all-too-frequent train wrecks that the papers gave catch labels to, like The Angola Horror—Brandon had barely averted one that would have merited such a name last year—and the extortion John B. Parker and his like practiced with rates, Brandon saw that an argument could be made that railroads were more trouble than they were worth. "Would you want to go all the way to the Exposition, all the way to Philadelphia, on horseback or in a buggy?"

"If I could," Ed Marks said gloomily. "But I don't see that I can ever do that."

Brandon's shirt and drawers felt scratchy on his freshly laundered skin. He wondered if the hot soak in the bathhouse behind Danby's had worn away an armor of grime and old skin, or if the fresh garments were just stiff from having been folded away in his valise.

Waiting in the barbershop for a shave from Danby as the culmination of his grooming, Brandon studied the *Leslie's* he had picked up from the table next to his chair. Not unexpectedly, the front page was lavish with engravings of the Exposition, exotic buildings that appeared to be the pavilions of such countries as China, Turkey, and

Egypt, and a remarkable room that imitated a limestone cave bristling with stalactites and stalagmites, reminiscent of the one he had been trapped in in Arizona—the second reminder of past adventures this afternoon.

Browsing among the illustrations, he was surprised to see that above the entrance to what he took to be the main building a large sign read "Grande Porte." He looked for the first time at the text, and then at the date of the magazine, and discovered that the exposition he was studying was that held in Paris in 1867.

The way it has to be, Counselor, is that when the rag men or whoever pick up newspapers when you're done with them, they take them to a warehouse someplace and hold on to them a minimum of five years, and then they take and sell them to barbershops and dentists' offices and the like at cheap prices. It's a rag man's oath they take, like the Masons. That's why all the magazines and weeklies you see are old. As Geary would say, it's the only thing that makes sense.

Wen Hing agreed to starch the shirts and collars just enough to give them body, stopping well short of the sheet-metal effect that overenthusiastic laundrymen tended to try for, and to employ no starch whatever on the drawers and socks. Helen Kitson would have been willing to deal with Brandon's laundry, but he did not want to add to her work. Also, it had been his observation that women and men approached laundry differently, with women being intractable about starch and inclined to produce neat, crisp creases where current custom did not demand them. The memory was still green of a pair of summer trousers an aunt had laundered for him when he was sixteen, starched so that he had to force his feet into them to the accompaniment of a loud crackling sound.

Wen Hing was either only modestly fluent in English or preferred to confine his conversation to professional matters; in any case, a little to Brandon's surprise, he did not confess his longing to make his way to Philadelphia to delight in the exhibits the emperor of his lost homeland had sent.

The last town errand Brandon had was the amendment of a pinch that had developed in the left shoe of his spare pair. Antonelli's shop was next to the laundry, and he entered to find the shoemaker at his last.

Antonelli said that the shoe would be as supple and comfortable as glove leather by the next day. "Ay hear they got a big building all for shyoes and leather at the Exposition, machines for doing everything with shyoes, maybe even a machine for soften them."

"The way everybody talks about it, I'm coming to think there's nothing the Exposition doesn't have," Brandon said. "I wonder what Columbus would think if he came back to life and dropped in on Philadelphia."

"Columbus?"

Brandon looked at the shoemaker. "Man who discovered America?"

Antonelli shook his head. "Leif Eriksson, Ay always heard."

Brandon was astonished by Carl Swanson's photographs of the frontier. As the man in Edwards's store had said, they had a vivid realism about them that made them seem almost three-dimensional. They contrasted strongly with the portraits ranged on the walls of the shop, samples of his local work, and Swanson caught Brandon's quick glance at those.

"Yeah, they're not as good," Swanson said. "Flat, stiff. When I settled here and got to doing portraits regular I did them like the other work, tried to make them really good pictures. But the customers didn't like it. They couldn't quite say why, but one of 'em said her picture wasn't dignified. I think for these folks a photograph is something formal and solemn, a little like the look people get at you in your coffin."

"Lifelike, not alive, huh?" Brandon said. He wondered what one of Carl Swanson's "really good" photographs of himself would look like, one that would tell as much about him as the prints in front of him did about the scenes they depicted, and felt strongly that he would not want to see it.

The one he was looking at now showed the view out and down from a mountain range: a basin of open land with a winding stream running through it, and a distant house with a patch of dark vegetation around it; on the right, the curving heights of the upthrust mountains where the camera stood; ahead, the massive shoulder of another mountain pushing out of the earth. The evidences of vegetable and human life in the center of the picture seemed frail and irrelevant, ready to be wiped from the everlasting rock. Brandon had not looked on that actual scene, but the awe and the sense of pettiness of even the most intense human concerns it evoked— those he had felt, and had to suppress, too many times.

"A few years ago I couldn't have got that," Carl Swanson said. "Anyplace a wagon for the darkroom and carrying the equipment couldn't go, you couldn't take a picture. And even now a damned heavy camera and a bunch of glass plates, it's a load. If they ever find a way to put the emulsion on paper instead of glass, and to make the camera lighter, I could get pictures you wouldn't believe. On the other hand, it'd make it so easy, everybody'd do it, and nobody'd pay photographers any more. That one you're looking at goes with the next. I don't know how I was crazy enough to stay still long enough to take it."

Brandon held a print showing a broad reach of prairie with a knife-edge horizon; the sky was light far off but darkened to near-blackness overhead. A wide-mouthed funnel hung from the darkness, hazy at the top, but gaining a dreadful clarity as it narrowed and reached down to nose at the ground. A farmhouse near a clump of trees was in the left foreground between the cyclone and the camera.

"It doesn't show in the picture, but there was lightning in the damn thing," Carl Swanson said.

Brandon took up the next picture. It was the same

scene, though the sky was considerably lighter. The trees were still there, but they were now next to what looked like a pile of jackstraws, one of which pierced a tree trunk.

"The folks inside came through that," Carl Swanson said. "Hid in the cyclone cellar whilst the house got turned to scrap lumber above 'em."

Brandon paused at a photograph of a broad trail of pulverized earth with prairie grasses on either side, a horned skull catching the sun whitely, and far ahead a cloud of dust and indistinctly seen shapes of horses, riders, and walking cattle. He could almost feel the heat and the dust in the back of his throat, the time he had ridden past the river of cattle and their attendant cowboys that made up the first trail drive he had seen, and turned for a final look as it moved on north. The camera might have been sitting on his shoulder at that very moment.

And this tightly composed picture of railroad tracks gleaming liquidly in the sun, their rigidly determined curve a mocking visual echo of the looser curve of the rock-bedded stream behind it, nested between steep forested slopes, said what he had felt in Colorado, riding along the tracks that had penetrated the ancient wilderness only days before.

As Brandon picked up each new print, glossy on its stiff paper, it seemed to him almost as if he were attending a magic lantern show of his travels in search of Gren Kenneally and the rest. Here was a river steamboat, if not on the lower Colorado, on a muddy, shallow river much like it; a shabby, violent cow town, the violence suggested by a man lying facedown in the dirt street and faces at windows or in the shadows of doorways; a bare hill rising like a stone wave, mutilated with mine shafts and open pits and scabbed with randomly placed ramshackle buildings; ruins of an Indian city under a pale full moon, different in detail but as eerie as Yehala, site of a carving like the self-swallowing, self-birthing snake on his coin.

The bell in the front of the shop clanked. "You go on looking while I see to that," Carl Swanson said, and he left the back room.

The next picture in the group Brandon took for a moment to be of a pavilion at some exposition, a tall building with a curving, three-layered tiled roof; then the huddle of buildings around it and the sharp zigzag of a telegraph wire located it in a big city's Chinatown, almost certainly San Francisco. It could even have been the headquarters of Tsai Wang, the tong chief who wanted Gren Kenneally dead as much as Brandon did.

He turned over the next photograph and nearly dropped it. This was clearly San Francisco, the ornamented facade of the Bella Union melodeon at Washington and Kearny. Brandon remembered it well, and had passed a few evenings experiencing the rowdy entertainment it offered, thinking that it might attract Gren Kenneally if he were still in the city. Perhaps Brandon had been right about the place if not the time; the bulky, eagle-beaked figure leaning against the front of the building and regarding the camera, or the world in general, with a disdainful malignance, fit all the descriptions of Gren Kenneally that Brandon had been given. When he saw the long, lined face behind the powerful nose, it was as familiar as Elise's, though he had never seen it. He took in a long, shuddering breath and let it rush out. A coincidence, they happened all the time—if you take a picture in a city, there will be people in it, and one of those people could be a murdering maniac called Kenneally. Everybody has to be some place, and Gren Kenneally was in this place and so was Carl Swanson with his camera. You could think of it as practically inevitable. . . .

Brandon lifted his head to call to Carl Swanson, then stopped himself. What could Swanson tell him? Only when the picture was taken, and that was merely fact, not useful information. He knew Gren Kenneally had been in San Francisco, and knew when he had left. The photograph was a slice of preserved time, faded like a plant pressed in an album, in no way a link to the Gren Kenneally of somewhere and now.

But he touched the smooth surface of the print and felt a tingle, as if it held an electric charge, as he sometimes felt when he touched the Indian coin in his pocket.

There was one picture remaining from the stack, and Brandon was reluctant to turn it over, like a faro player who knows that his stake will be won or lost when the hock card is revealed. Finally he did so, and felt relieved.

It was merely a landscape, with no pagodas or murderers to lend it drama. It hardly seemed to need it, though. It showed in the distance a high waterfall, partly hidden by sheer faces of rock plunging down the right side of the print into a roiling river that sped from the foot of the fall and out the bottom of the picture. It funneled between the slabs of rock to the right and a formation that swelled like an upthrusting thumb to the left, topped with a jagged peak atop an overhang suspended above the rushing water like a balcony. In the far background, an implacable, fluted rockface stood like a wall guarding a city of giants.

Brandon looked at the scene with growing intensity. It was picturesque in the extreme, certainly, but . . . there was something else about it, something that made the stern masses of rock and the compressed torrent below in some way horrible, as if they were a setting for a drama too large and too bloody for any stage.

He did not know how he knew it, perhaps Swanson had said something earlier, or perhaps he had seen the same scene in an engraving in a magazine or book, but he was certain it was in the Yellowstone Park, that wild tract larger than the two smallest states put together. For a moment he had an impulse to slide the picture into his pocket, then stifled it, wondering what compulsion had made him almost commit a pointless and unforgivable theft.

Brandon set the picture down, confused and troubled. The sight of Gren Kenneally's photographed face—if it was truly his—and the pictures so closely resembling the places he had been in reminded him that he was making no progress with what had brought him to Bigsbee, except the negative progress of ruling out one not very likely prospect, the discouraged farmer Harney. Worse, he was spending more thought and energy on selling Nonpareil's windmills than on hunting for Farmer Dick, letting Calvin Blake become the reality, not the mask, as Ned Norland had warned.

But then Edmund Chambers, the old itinerant actor, had given him advice that had worked well: believe you *are* the character you're playing, and the audience will go along. So far Brandon had done well enough following both men's advice, Ned Norland's for tracking and survival, Edmund Chambers's for disguise. Were they now in conflict? The only thing to do, probably, was follow whichever course seemed to be working. And at the moment, nothing was.

He set the stack of photographs back on the shelf from which Carl Swanson had taken them and in doing so dislodged a cloth tucked into the shelf. This revealed another, shorter pile of photographs tied with a ribbon. The sound of Swanson's voice came from the front of the shop, and he seemed to be in an extended conversation with his customer.

Maybe the ones that aren't worth showing? Brandon wondered. But if he's that good, even his second-rate stuff should be interesting. He untied the ribbon and turned over the first photograph.

Not second-rate, but highly interesting. Brandon had seen paintings and statues of naked women, as well as actual naked women. He had not, as far as he could recall, seen a photograph of one. This was, like Carl Swanson's other work, vivid and immediate. It showed the woman, half sitting, half leaning on one arm, in a grassy meadow, facing away from the camera. Some distance away was a farmhouse, and beyond it the swell of hill and farmland and a wide, empty sky.

The farmhouse was recognizable to Brandon, and so, in spite of the turned-away face, was the tumbled hair and the tense attitude of the body.

The next picture made it certain. Standing thigh-deep in a creek, joyously facing the camera and the sun, her ripe body diamonded with drops of water, Helen Kitson looked almost precisely as she had this morning in his unbidden vision of her bathing.

Brandon quickly retied the bundle of photographs, returned it to the shelf, replaced the concealing cloth, and took the original set of pictures out again. Helen Kitson's notion of an "understanding" encompassed a bit more than he had expected, well beyond holding hands at a church social. And the way she had been looking at the camera, presumably at the man operating it, suggested that Carl Swanson was a very lucky man, and that his luck had been demonstrated very soon after the shutter had snapped.

Before he could turn his mind away completely from what he had just seen, a vagrant thought drifted across it that had no business in Calvin Blake's mind, or Cole Brandon's: A damn shame they won't have anything like that at the women's pavilion at the Centennial. . . .

12

Swicegood pulled the lever that released the catch holding the wheel still (called the catch release lever in the book of instructions; Nonpareil prided itself on clarity), and the wind took the slats and sent the wheel whirling on its axle. The crank set the pumpshaft moving, the pump gurgled horribly for long enough to set a tide of dismay rising in Brandon, and then water spat out of the pump mouth and began flowing in a steady stream into the large wooden tank Swicegood had built in advance.

Swicegood, Brandon, Walter Kitson, and Swicegood's three nearest neighbors watched the steady stream of water the mill was summoning from the earth. All of them were sweaty and smeared with dust and earth from having labored to bolt the heavy mill to the precon-structed tower and then, with the aid of two teams of Swicegood's horses, hauled it upright and completed the final connection to the pump.

"My God," Swicegood said. "All that water, like a river coming out of the ground. Way my land lies, I can dig ditches from here, send water all through my crops when they need it, let the stock water as they want."

Brandon looked up at the whirling sunflower face of the mill and said, a good deal more matter-of-factly than he felt, "That's what the Nonpareil's for, Mr. Swicegood." The whole business, seen up close, seemed as much like a miracle to him as it did to Swicegood.

Walter Kitson and the other farmers murmured and commented, listening to the water splashing into the tank. Brandon gauged from their tone that he had a pretty good chance of selling at least a couple of windmills among them.

Doran, one of the farmers, drew Brandon aside and said, "It's a wonder, sure enough. But cash is always a problem, even something down and the rest on time. Any chance of shading the price some?"

"None," Brandon said firmly. Charging full price to Swicegood and less to others would be disastrous. "Mr. Rattner at the bank thinks these machines make good farming sense and good business sense, and I believe he'd listen if you wanted to talk about a loan to buy one."

"Well, by God, maybe I will," Doran said. "Walter's goin' in to Bigsbee right from here, and I'll catch a ride with him. You come see me tomorrow, Blake, and we can maybe talk more about it."

Another neighbor expressed almost as much interest, and Brandon made a note to call on him right after seeing Doran. Doran would, Brandon hoped, spread word of the windmill's dramatic performance around Bigsbee; and so, he guessed, would Walter Kitson in the course of his errands in Bigsbee.

Driving away from the farm and relishing in anticipation the pleasure of sprawling on his bed and resting the back, arm, and shoulder muscles that had been harder tried than in some time, Brandon looked back over his shoulder.

The windmill rose on its slender tower, whirling briskly. The light wind was steady from the northwest, and the vane was motionless, displaying its picture of a morose sachem and the proud gilt-lettered legend KICK-APOO INDIAN SAGWA.

"I'm glad Walter went on into town and you didn't, Mr. Blake," Helen Kitson said, "for I want to talk to somebody."

Brandon abandoned the idea of repose on his bed; the kitchen chair was comfortable enough. He was a little surprised not to find it a touch embarrassing to talk to Helen Kitson after having seen those pictures of her a few days ago, but he was in fact more at ease with her than before. It was as if he knew her well, which in a way he did, and also as if he need not be curious about what her worn dress and apron hid; that he remembered in every detail.

"Talk about what, Miss Helen?"

"Have you met any nice women in town?"

"Ah . . . I—well, I haven't been looking for any nice women. Or, uh . . ."

"The other kind? No, I didn't mean for yourself," Helen Kitson said. "I mean sort of around the town, women that look like they had some sense and good spirits. You see, I don't get to town much, and when I'm there I don't mix with the ladies, for I'm not in any sewing circle or church groups, not having the time." Brandon could tell, judging by the photographs he had seen—and the others in the stack that he now regretted not having looked at—that how Helen Kitson spent the spare time she did have was a good deal more absorbing than what Bigsbee's female social circles could offer.

"I thought maybe some of the men there might have had a sister or a sister-in-law or some such say hello to you, a new gentleman in town," Helen Kitson said.

Brandon shook his head. "No introductions, not even to mothers-in-law."

"Darn," Helen Kitson said. She looked at the wide boards of the kitchen floor and then up at Brandon. "I want to get a wife for Walter, that's what he needs here. What I said the other day, and a while before that, about the loneliness and the wind and the hard work, it's true, but it makes a difference if you're doing it for your man, the other half of a partnership. Doing it for a nephew, that comes to feel as if there's no use to it after a while, even though it's got to be done, and it gets so you only see the bad side of it. I've come to see why it is women work so hard, Mr. Blake. Somehow, sometime, they got the responsibility for keeping things going laid on them, and they keep at it 'cause nobody else will do it."

"That's what happened to you, Counselor, he thought. There was a responsibility laid on you, and nobody else is going to see to it. Like they say about women's work, it looks as if it's never done.

"Anyhow, a wife for Walter would make things better all around. He'd have a woman to do for him, and I'd be free to . . ."

"Get on with that understanding you told me of," Brandon said.

"Yes," Helen Kitson said with a throaty undertone that vividly evoked the happily wanton glance she directed at the camera as she stood in the stream.

"Um, Walter doesn't know a thing about that, your understanding, does he?" Brandon said. He had not thought about it, but Walter Kitson's manner to Carl Swanson was not the one he would have adopted toward a known suitor of his aunt—leaving aside the photographs and the kind of courtship they indicated.

"No, he doesn't. He's awful strict, Walter is, and if there was any kind of attachment betwixt me and a gentleman, Walter'd have us married in no time or turn me out of the house, and then the farm would go to rack and ruin without a woman to see to it. And that wouldn't be fair to Walter, and it'd be letting my poor brother down, that worked so hard to get the place going."

"I'm sorry I can't help," Brandon said. "I will keep my eyes open when I'm in town, even ask if there's a nice schoolteacher or storekeeper that's new here."

"That'd be kind," Helen Kitson said. "And it'd be a favor, too, if you had a word with my gentleman friend.

Sometimes he's a little careless about meeting me, and I'm afraid we might get known about, and it would get back to Walter, and there'd be an almighty fuss. Would you do that, suggest he . . ."

"Exercise more discretion?"

"Just so," Helen Kitson said. "Being a salesman does give you such a lot of words that you've always got the one you need to hand, don't it?"

"Glad to do it," Brandon said. "Who's the fortunate man?"

She gave him a level look. "Why, a long-headed gentleman like you, Mr. Blake, you'll have figured that out a while ago."

On the way to his room Brandon reflected that it had stopped surprising him that women knew things they couldn't possibly know; but he had yet to arrive at any theory of *how* they knew it. Whatever the explanation was, he was sure there would not be a trace of it at the women's pavilion at the Exposition.

The buggy's wheels still turned smoothly with no trace of a wobble days after Ed Marks's repair work, and Brandon decided not to stop at the livery stable this trip. Carl Swanson's store was just past the next cross street, and he flapped the reins in a slow-down signal and guided the horse toward the side of the street.

What in particular was menacing about the sudden blur of motion at the head of the side street he could never afterwards say; but even as his corner-eye vision registered it he was rolling sideways out of the buggy.

The fabric of the vehicle's top turned to shreds and its wooden frame splintered as a load of shot blasted through it. Brandon's leap had landed him crouching just to the rear of the still-moving buggy, and he dived to the dirt surface of the street in time for the shotgun's second barrel to discharge over him and produce a crash of glass and a howl of pain and horror behind him.

Without thought or will his legs flexed and propelled him toward the figure holding the shotgun and jamming a shell into the opened breech. He crashed into the man, bowling him over, grabbing him, then finding himself squeezed by powerful arms and almost choked by acrid animal smell with a sour overlay that was peculiarly and repellently human. Jere Sublette, then, not that there was anyone else it would have been.

He wrenched an arm loose and grabbed at Sublette's face. This was the kind of fight in which eye-gouging was an acceptable procedure, if you could find the eye.

Brandon found himself up on one knee, with his left hand still free, and drove a punch into Sublette's nose that slammed his head against the ground. Then he saw rushing booted feet and grabbing, striking hands, felt Sublette's grip relax, and was lifted to his feet.

Edwards, Carl Swanson, and four other men were holding the dazed and sagging Sublette. They and the throng that was forming around them exchanged astonished glances. For once the men of Bigsbee had acted together to face Jere Sublette, and they had brought him down. They had always accepted that they could not do that, and now, in the space of seconds, it was done.

Ed Marks provided the length of rope that bound Jere Sublette's arms to his sides as he was marched to the jail. The men who had fought him and those who had watched the fight—except for the luckless bystander whose leg had intercepted several pellets from the shotgun's second barrel and who was now being mined by the doctor—formed a ragged procession of escort, now headed by chief of police Hodge, who had not contributed to the proceedings but who did have the key to the jail.

A sort of music was provided for the parade by Jere Sublette, who kept up a maniacal roar of cursing, threats, and boasting that was as loud and gut-wrenching as any band drum section.

"No man don't use Jere Sublette like no animal, God rot yer balls! Loosen me up an' I'll rip the throats outen every one o' ye, hands behint my back, ye weasels, skunks, scorpions! Gimme a fair chanst an' I'll stuff yer heads up yer asses an' let ye chew on yer own livers!"

The tirade echoed from the fronts of the houses they passed, and Brandon realized that it would carry some distance, well into the north edge and the environs of the Seagull. He slipped his gun from his trousers and moved toward the north side of Main Street, up which Sublette was still being marched. He saw that Ed Marks and a few other men had also taken up flanking positions on that side of Sublette's escorting group, which was now enlarged by more spectators, several boys and dogs, and a few women.

No rescuing force appeared from the direction of the north edge, though, and, as empty lots began to appear among the houses toward the town's outskirts, Brandon moved over to walk next to Ed Marks.

"Jail's not very central," he said.

Marks pointed toward a boxy one-story structure a hundred yards in front of them. "Just ahead. Way I heard, when they set up the town they figured the jail would be mostly for drunks, and most drunks get noisy sometimes. So they decided to build it out this way, where the poor part of town would grow up, and the noise wouldn't bother anybody but the riffraff. But the bad district grew up to the north, not the west, so the jail's out here on its ownsome. Anyhow, Sublette can make all the noise he wants, and it won't trouble nobody but the coyotes and the prairie dogs."

Brandon and the others watched as Sublette, with four guns held inches from his head, was unwrapped from his cocoon of rope, thrust inside the wooden cube, constructed of heavy timbers, and locked in behind its massive door.

"I got a spare buggy top," Ed Marks said. "Bring yours in, and I'll replace the one that crazy bastard shot away. Sublette really had it in for you, didn't he?" He grimaced. "There ain't nothing scarier than a crazy man. And if it's a crazy man with a gun, it's the worst it can get. You come out of it lucky, Mr. Blake."

Elise and the rest came up against a crazy man with a gun, Brandon thought, and they weren't lucky. Was Sublette one of Gren's gang? he wondered. The farmer stuff docsn't fit, but a lot of the rest does. And if I did find out it was him, what then? Marks is right, he's crazy, madhouse crazy. No court would let him stand trial, no jurisdiction would execute him, not that I give a damn about that.

But if he's insane, can *I* execute him?

13

Brandon wondered if it was market day, or if perhaps somebody was selling special-price Centennial Exposition excursion tickets. Main Street, where it ran through the main business blocks, was thronged with people gathering in knots and talking with considerable animation and arm-waving, breaking off from one knot and rushing to another and talking and gesticulating again. He had hoped to have a brief trip into town, collecting his laundry and shoes, seeing if Ed Marks could replace the buggy top quickly, and passing Helen Kitson's message on to Carl Swanson. Yesterday, after the shotgun attack and Jere Sublette's jailing, had not seemed the right time for that, but it looked as if his stay in Bigsbee might consume some time.

He stopped the buggy and got out of it well short of the milling crowd and walked toward Swanson's store. The photographer was outside on the street and waved Brandon over.

"Sublette's busted out!" he said.

"That jail looked pretty solid," Brandon said, "and a damned heavy-looking lock on the door."

"It is, but what it looks like, some of them from the

113

north edge, his pals, they came down and took the hinge pins off the door and got Sublette out."

"Where's he gone?" Brandon said.

"Nobody knows." Brandon turned and nodded at Simon Rattner, who had come up to join their talk. "Nobody's had sight of him, though there's word just come in that he might have burned out some farmer he's got a grudge against, man named Harney. Anyhow, Harney's place burned down last night."

"Harney say it was him?" Carl Swanson asked.

Simon Rattner shook his head. "He hasn't been seen. Maybe scared off, or maybe Sublette did for him."

More likely, Brandon thought, that Harney had finally gone off, admitting failure to himself but to no one else and, as he had said he might, leaving only ashes as a memorial.

Brandon heard Geary's excited voice from more than twenty feet away: "Damn it, you let him get away from you, and now you're not doing anything about catching him!" He was, Brandon saw, talking to Chief Hodge.

"Didn't get away from *me,*" Hodge said defensively. "His friends or whoever, they got him out of the jail. I'm not the jailer."

"There *isn't* a jailer!" Geary said.

"That's why it was so easy to get him out," the police chief said. "But if the town don't pay for a jailer, then they don't get a jailer. As for doing anything, I'd say Bigsbee's better off without Jere Sublette, in jail or out of it. He's gone, and if he keeps on going, I say good riddance."

Most of the men gathered around Geary and Hodge seemed to agree with that view, but Geary continued to fulminate and emit incoherent ideas for pursuing Sublette, like a stale firework sending off sputtering sparks and smoke.

With no further sensation to feed it the crowd dispersed, and Brandon collected his laundry from Wen Hing (the collars smooth and firm, but satisfactorily soft) and his shoe from Antonelli (comfortable, when he tried it on, as a well-broken-in slipper). He left the buggy with Ed Marks and doubled back on Main to Carl Swanson's shop.

"I was talking to Miss Helen Kitson the other day," Brandon said, by way of starting a conversation he had no clear plan for.

"You would, her being your landlady," Carl Swanson said.

"Not about that kind of thing. Something particular," Brandon said.

"Miss Helen's a fine lady. Must be a pleasure to talk to her."

"It is, of course," Brandon said. "But, uh, she was talking about, well, being careful."

"Carelessness makes a lot of trouble," Carl Swanson said. "You work with glass plates and acid, the way I do, and you learn to be careful. I would think Miss Helen is a careful lady."

"Oh, she is," Brandon said. "But not everybody else is, and she told me that worried her some, people not being careful about, uh, things. To her way of thinking, that's how things get known that shouldn't be known, when people aren't careful."

"It would seem so," Carl Swanson said. "It's a sad thing when somebody's business becomes everybody's business, and taking care's the best way to see it don't." He waited to see if Brandon had anything more to say in that vein, then said, "Have you sold any more windmills? I think the Pe-Ru-Na company would pay a little extra to get an ad up on one."

Brandon left the shop unsure if he had conveyed Helen Kitson's request for discretion clearly and if he had received any assurances in return—and if, in fact, he had not conducted the whole conversation with so much discretion that no actual information had been transmitted or received.

He was at the livery stable, admiring the deftness with which Ed Marks was fastening a salvaged top to the buggy—fancier than the one Jere Sublette's shotgun blast had shredded, as it had an isinglass window at the back, which Brandon supposed was an improvement if you worried about what might be coming up behind you—when he heard shouts and the sound of running feet. Amid the confused voices he caught the word "Sublette."

He and Ed Marks stepped into the street and found the scene much as it had been an hour earlier, with knots of vehement talkers, the largest and most agitated one surrounding Chief Hodge and his constable, Lunney.

Simon Rattner, calmer than the men around him, said, "Well, you're right, Chief, it wouldn't do for you and Lunney to go there after him, there's too many of his crowd for you. We can wire the sheriff in Platteville, and he can have his men here in a couple of hours, either riding or on the afternoon train."

"Some folks saw Sublette at an upstairs window at the Seagull," Edwards muttered to Brandon and Ed Marks. "And Hodge said flat out that getting him out of there was a job beyond what he and Lunney was paid for." Brandon agreed. Most of the denizens of the north edge he had seen looked furtive and weedy, but an army of coyotes could pull down a panther, and if they chose to defend Sublette, a two-man police force could not do much about it.

"No!" Geary shouted. "Sublette's a Bigsbee problem, and it's Bigsbee men'll settle it! We don't need to run whining to Platteville for a sheriff to wipe our noses. We'll by damn handle this our own selves!"

"Yeah," said Danby, who was holding a shaving mug in one hand and standing next to a man with a face partly covered with soap foam, "we go in there and get him, and next as you know we show up at Platteville and turn him over to the sheriff all ready for trying. That'll show them in Platteville that Bigsbee ain't no back number."

Murmurs from the crowd indicated a consensus inclining toward Geary's view as supported by Danby—as Brandon now remembered, a town council member—and even Simon Rattner appeared to be considering it.

Brandon supposed that the citizens of a town like Bigsbee, with not much to boast of these days, might well feel that calling in outside help to deal with even a malefactor of demonic proportions was a humiliation they would take some risks to shun. Having delivered him up for trial, though, what would the charges be? Property damage and minor wounding with a firearm would be the only clearly provable ones, and Brandon wondered if they would net enough of a sentence to make the whole business worthwhile. The best thing would have been if the men who had spotted Sublette had told Chief Hodge only, and the Chief, if he knew his business, would have gotten word to Sublette that a sudden and unobtrusive flight would not result in pursuit.

"We better do it right now!" Geary bawled. "Sublette's up there planning to burn the whole town and loot it, just like he burned out poor Harney's place and left his charred corpse in the ashes!" The vividness of this picture seemed to obscure the fact that there was only a rumor of a fire at Harney's farm and not even a rumor of his death by incineration or any other means. Geary appeared to have discovered the demagogue's secret, that the most unfounded assertion can persuade a crowd if it is made firmly enough; it was probably, Brandon thought, not a result of study but a fortuitous consequence of monomania.

"Harney told me he was thinking of pulling stakes and burning his place, and my guess is he's done it," Brandon told Ed Marks and Edwards.

"Likely enough," Ed Marks said. "But I think Geary's got the crowd with him now, and saying that wouldn't do much but get you tagged as being on Sublette's side."

"It's a dumb idea," Edwards said. "But I'm joining in, and I'd suggest you fellows do, too, for if enough men with sense don't, it'll be only fools going after Sublette, and God knows what'd happen then."

Fools, sensible men, and whoever fell between the extremes milled for a while in the street; then, under the suggestions, commands, and proddings of a few who found themselves giving orders and being listened to, they formed into a kind of platoon and moved off toward the north edge of town. Those who were carrying weapons pulled them from holster or pocket and held them ready for use. Some, as the procession passed their homes or places of business, would break ranks and dart inside, emerging armed; others would turn aside to pick up a heavy length of wood or even a rock. Brandon found himself near the front, acting as a kind of marshal or shepherd. Chief Hodge and Simon Rattner were where the leaders would be if there were any, giving some color of legality to the posse. Constable Lunney was back in the pack, next to the newspaper editor and publisher, Kingslake. Brandon was interested to note that Geary seemed content to be part of the group. Once he had started the whole enterprise in motion he did not seem to be interested in directing it.

As they moved through Bigsbee's back streets Brandon could see occasional running figures ahead of them; full word of what was happening was being conveyed to the north edge, and certainly to the Seagull and Jere Sublette's friends and supporters.

The Seagull loomed over the hovels around it, its second story visible before they turned a corner and came in sight of the front of the building. Half a dozen or more men were grouped around the door, blocking it and facing the oncoming marchers. Brandon saw no weapons openly displayed, but several men had their arms crossed or resting on their belts, and it was a safe bet that most of them could have guns out and aimed within an eyeblink.

"Stand aside," Chief Hodge said.

The man squarely in the doorway wore a white apron that identified him as the bartender. Brandon, standing next to Hodge, could see that he was about evenly divided between truculence and apprehension. "This is private property, admittance to customers only, and we got more customers than we can handle right now, so there's no room, and you can go away."

"We're coming in, the good citizens of this town, and

118

you'd best stand out of the way, Jack Gannon," Chief Hodge said.

"The hell you're coming in, and why the hell would you want to?" Gannon said.

"We've come for Jere Sublette," the chief said.

"Jere's long gone from here," Gannon said.

"Seen here not an hour ago, at that upstairs window." Hodge pointed over Gannon's head.

Gannon shook his head. "That's not possible if he's not here," he said.

"Are you calling me a liar?"

Brandon caught a flicker of motion at the center second-story window and got an impression of a bearded, glaring face. So did others in the crowd, and one man called out, "No, it's goddamn Jere hisself givin' you the lie, Gannon! Showed his mug right over yer lyin' face!"

Gannon's face twisted in disgust an instant before the men at the front of the extralegal posse pushed him aside and burst into the saloon. Brandon did not know who had started the assault but found himself in it, with Hodge, Ed Marks, and three other men. They ran through the deserted barroom and to the flight of stairs at its back. Pounding up the stairs behind Chief Hodge, Brandon held his revolver loosely, the barrel angled well outward, and earnestly hoped that the men behind him were being equally careful.

At the top of the stairs there were four rooms off a corridor that ran the length of the building, and a door at the front end, clearly leading to the room Sublette had peered out from.

Ed Marks, the first to reach the door, kicked it open, plunged into the room, and continued the plunge into the far wall, propelled by a chair Jere Sublette smashed over his head. The five others swarmed into the room and grabbed or struck at Sublette. Brandon pocketed his revolver and aimed a blow at Sublette's jaw; this was too close quarters for gunplay.

Sublette briefly shook his attackers loose like a bear

119

beset by hounds, then was driven to the wall as they surged over him again. Brandon had a grip on one arm and was trying to bend it the wrong way when Sublette convulsed and hurled himself backward, landing against the window, which shattered without impeding his progress. Brandon let go just in time not to be pulled out with him and poked his head out the emptied window frame, carefully steering around the glass daggers at its edge.

Sublette was lying face up, seemingly stunned, with the lower portion of one of the posse protruding from under his massive body, heels drumming frantically. The crowd surged over Sublette, hauling him to stand upright but with lolling head and gaping mouth.

For a moment the group of angry, excited men and their quarry formed a tableau; no one moved or spoke, and the only sound was Sublette's rasping breathing.

Then someone—Brandon thought Geary, but the voice was an animal howl, unidentifiable—yelled, "Hang him! Hang the murdering bastard!"

Chief Hodge pushed Brandon aside and leaned out the window, careless of the fragment of glass that cut into the side of his head. "No! You can't do that! We've got to—"

"He's wounded the chief!" "Chief's dyin!" "Hang him!" "Hang him!" "Hang him!"

Hodge was clearly debating a leap from the window into the crowd to stop the hanging. To Brandon it looked like a clear invitation to a broken leg, and he turned and ran from the room and down the corridor and into Ed Marks, who had recovered enough to stumble away from the scene of the fight, but not enough to navigate competently.

He clutched Brandon and said, "What happened, Blake?"

"Sublette skulled you with a chair, went out the window, and now they're going to hang him—I'm going down to try to stop it."

An elated yell came from the crowd outside. Sounds like someone found a rope, Brandon thought.

"Oh, thass no good," Ed Marks said fuzzily. "Jere's a

shit, but no call to hang for that, lots an' lots needin' t' be hanged 'fore you get to the likes of Jere. We oughta stoppit."

Brandon brushed past him, but Marks revived enough to be close behind him at the head of the stairs. Brandon started down them two at a time, then heard a startled grunt behind him and a skid of booted feet, and he took the impact of Ed Marks's falling body on his back and thighs.

The stairs and the barroom floor tilted up to meet him; a flung arm protected his face from the impact of the stair risers, but his body jolted down them like a piece of soap being abraded on a giant washboard. He bounced off the last step and hit the floor with Marks sprawled half on top of him; his revolver, jounced from his pocket, spun across the floor, wobbling on its cylinder.

As Brandon scrambled to his feet he heard a roar from outside. It was something like the noise of a crowd he had heard at a cockfight once, when the winner's spur sank to its full length in the loser's head and the match was over: approving, exultant, conclusive, and, heard while standing apart from it, profoundly shaming.

He walked to the door, sensing that there was no need to run. To see the avid faces of the crowd, staring at a point just above his head, he had to look past a pair of cracked and broken boots swaying in front of him at eye level.

He edged past them and looked up. Jere Sublette, eyes wide and tongue protruding in a parody of defiance, head almost resting on one shoulder, glared down from where he dangled from the end of a rope slung over the bracket supporting the spread-winged white wooden bird over the Seagull's door.

From a distance, Brandon thought, the scene might look like a religious pageant, with the bird about to lift Sublette into heaven to the gaping astonishment of the multitude.

14

And then the whole bunch of them went to the burying ground, out beyond the jail, and they dug a grave at the edge of it, not really in it with the properly buried folks, but right against it, and they wrapped him in a tarpaulin somebody had, and they buried him, and that was the end of it." Brandon sat back in the straight-backed chair and stared into the flickering fan-shaped flame of the coal-oil lantern on the Kitsons' kitchen table. You could have just as well said "we," Counselor, he thought, not "them." You didn't hold the rope for him, but you were there, and by being there you had a hand in it with the rest. If you could be sure he was Farmer Dick, there'd be an end to your reason for being here, and you could be on the train out tomorrow. No such luck—he could have been, but more likely not, and now no chance of proving it either way.

Brandon had not wanted to recount the day's events to Helen and Walter Kitson, but now that he had he felt a little lightened. Helen Kitson seemed shaken. "What a terrible thing for you, for those men."

"For Sublette," Walter Kitson said.

"No," Helen Kitson said. "Nothing's terrible for him now. But Mr. Blake'll be seeing it for a long time, and the men who did it, why, they may be puffed up about it now, and boasting how brave and decisive they acted. But Mr. Sublette'll be looking at them for lots of nights to come, and then they'll be looking at themselves every time they shave, and they'll come not to like who's looking back at them."

"The town's a cleaner place with Sublette out of it, that's an important thing," Walter Kitson said. "I won't deny it's troubling that it was done the way it was done, but Sublette was a disgrace and a danger to the peace of the town, whether or not there was anything to that business about him having it burned. He's a boil that had to be burst, and maybe now that's done, the pus that's left can drain out, for the wickedness and foul doings he encouraged are still there. If what the mob did today brings that about, it won't have been wasted, even if there was wickedness in it."

"I only saw the north edge a couple of times," Brandon said, "but it looked more poor and sort of discouraged than wicked to me."

"The north edge is a hotbed of drinking and gaming and fornication and lewdness," Walter Kitson said, "a canker of drunk men and shameless women flaunting their bodies."

Brandon could not repress the impulse to flick a glance at Helen Kitson, remembering the exuberantly unashamed photographs in Carl Swanson's back room, but he quickly looked away from her thoughtful gaze.

"Justified or not, horrible or not, the main thing is that it's done with," Brandon said.

The next morning, after calling at three farms and finding the owners absent on trips to Bigsbee, Brandon decided to pursue his rounds in town. It might be tempting to a prospect to realize that within an hour of saying yes he could get approval of a bank loan from

Simon Rattner and have the order off the wire in Chicago, with eager hands already preparing a brand-new Nonpareil for shipment.

In the back room of Edwards's store there was the usual coffeepot, but no coffee drinkers. Brandon poured himself a cup and poked his head out into the store area.

Edwards looked at him and nodded. "Most of the other men are at their stores and such today, or out at the north edge."

"How come?"

Though there were no customers in the store, Edwards came over to Brandon and spoke quietly. "Last night some of the men that was in the business yesterday, they got together and formed a vigilance committee."

"What for?" Brandon said. "Sublette's gone."

"Seems like a lot of folks are unhappy about the doings in the north edge," Edwards said. "Not a respectable place, all told."

"Fornication, drinking, and gambling?"

"Just so," Edwards said.

"There's a place like that in every town," Brandon said. "Gives you at least a chance of not having drinking, fornication, and gambling all over town."

"I think you're right about that," Edwards said. "And so do a lot of others. But there's some that don't agree, and that's who's started the committee up. They aim to clear the riffraff out of Bigsbee, and it seems they've started."

"Who's on the committee?" Brandon asked.

Edwards shook his head. "Geary for sure, for he's the one that's been telling what their decisions are. Five or six other men that met in secret someplace last night and set the committee up and started to work."

Brandon sipped at his coffee and said, "Work?"

"Yeah," Edwards said. "They went to Jack Gannon late at night, black cloth over their faces—mourning handkerchiefs from Geary's stock, I expect—and explained to him that he didn't own the Seagull anymore, for the committee was confiscating it and turning it over to the town council, and what they'll do with it I can't imagine. And since Gannon didn't have an occupation anymore, he was a vagrant with no visible means of support, and the committee was declaring all such to be unwelcome in Bigsbee, so he was invited to present himself at the railroad station in time to board the first eastbound train."

"Jesus," Brandon said. "He gave in to them?"

"He did what most men would do if they're surrounded by half a dozen masked men with guns that just that afternoon lynched a man, yeah," Edwards said.

The committee then visited some of the more prominent, or notorious, residents of the north edge and explained to them that their time in Bigsbee was up, repeating the invitation to visit the depot at their earliest convenience.

"A complete cleanup, then," Brandon said. "An end to wickedness and sin in Bigsbee, that's the guarantee now?"

"If you castrate the men, lock up the women, and pour salt in all the booze, maybe you'll make a dent in it," Edwards said. "All the north edge did was make a place to put it in."

Brandon left Edwards's store and walked to the station. The platform was crowded with about thirty men and women looking variously bewildered, enraged, fearful, or indifferent. Gannon, the Seagull's recent owner, appeared dazed, and a swollen eye and lip suggested the forcefulness of the persuasion the vigilance committee had employed to encourage him to vacate. The former north edgers stood close together or sat on bags, boxes, and bundles they had with them. Many were overdressed for the warm weather, wearing long coats or, from the padded aspect of their figures, extra trousers, shirts, or skirts; they figure it's safer to wear their spare clothes away than carry them in a package somebody can steal, Brandon supposed.

Four men wearing gun belts with holstered revolvers prominently displayed—something Brandon had not yet seen in Bigsbee—stood on the platform or leaned against the station's walls. They had no uniforms or badges, but their attitude, and the distance the crowd they surveyed kept from them, marked them as guards.

Beyond the platform the river rippled and flashed in the sunlight, running on quickly with a freedom that mocked both prisoners and guards.

In the street beyond the platform thirty or so men and a few women stood and talked among themselves, rarely looking at the huddled north edgers awaiting expulsion but seemingly held where they were by some sort of gravitational attraction to them. Brandon saw many of those who had been in the group that attacked the Seagull the day before, but many who had not. His first, and so far only, customer, Swicegood, was there, and so were a few of the farmers to whom he had sung the Nonpareil windmill's praises.

As good as a dogfight for gathering customers together, Brandon thought, and he walked over to Swicegood.

"The Nonpareil still doing the job?" he asked after exchanging greetings.

"Can't complain," Swicegood said. "Say, ain't this some doings, though, Blake?" He gestured toward the platform.

"Remarkable," Brandon said. "How much water would you say the pump brings up now?"

"Don't know the gallonage, but it's what I need, that's the main thing. D'you know, this is kind of like with the Injuns, ain't it? You put up with 'em till they get to being troublesome, and then you round 'em up and send 'em on their ways and leave it to civilized people to get on with good works and godly living."

"A lot like that, yeah," Brandon said. Just about as fair or lawful, he thought, and for the benefit of the same self-satisfied yahoos. Yahoos who happen to be my customers, though. . . . "I guess you'd be willing to let some of your friends and neighbors know how satisfied you are, then?"

"Writing out a testimonial letter, like them in the papers?" Swicegood said. "Why, I'd be happy to, talk it up as nice as you please. In fact, you could do it yourself, say what you like, and I'll sign it." After that, Brandon was not at all surprised when Swicegood looked at him alertly and said, "The going rate's all right with me, for I don't expect you folks are stingy. What's it come to?"

"I'll have to check with the home office," Brandon said. "What I had in mind for now was something simpler—you telling men you knew around here that the Nonpareil's doing a good job for you." A little infusion of Kickapoo money, Brandon thought sourly, and the honest tiller of the soil is corrupted, looking for the chance for profit in whatever comes along. Which, come to think of it, who doesn't?

"They can ask, I'll answer," Swicegood said curtly.

Circulating among the farmers he hoped to bring into the satisfied family of Nonpareil owners, he pointed out Swicegood as the man who could tell them truthfully, though without taking much time at it, of the benefits the windmill would bring.

Brandon's prospective customers gave him only polite attention, and he suspected they would hardly remember what he was telling them; their interest was clearly on what was probably the reason for their being in town at all, the exiles on the platform.

These now stirred slightly, like cattle responding to a change in the wind that signals an oncoming storm, and the guards straightened to stand more alertly.

In a moment the distant scream of a whistle came from the west, and as if the piercing sound had made his ears more sensitive, Brandon could hear the faint chuffing of a locomotive. It grew louder very gradually until it expanded into a rhythmic coughing roar that began to slow and diminish just as it reached its maximum intensity. The diamond-stacked engine slid, slowing, past most of the platform and stopped at the eastern end. Nobody stepped out of the three passenger cars except for the conductor, who stood on the stairs and looked in astonishment at the crowd, at least ten times the size of any contingent that had ever embarked at Bigsbee station.

One of the guards went over to him and began talking. The conductor replied vehemently, and Brandon caught the words "no tickets?" and "crazy!"

The guard kept on talking and reached out a hand, which the conductor grasped, visibly relaxing. It seemed to Brandon that he had seen a flicker of dull green at the end of the guard's hand before the conductor's closed on it. Evidently the conductor had decided to take the north edgers at a cut fare that would never figure in the company's books and trust that there were no railroad inspectors traveling on that run today.

The men and women on the platform scrambled aboard the train, the train pulled out—no waving from the spectators—and the platform was once again empty, with nothing to impede the view of the river flowing beyond it.

The crowd in the street began to disperse, and Brandon abandoned any idea of pursuing the farmers to press the claims of the Nonpareil; not the time for it.

The guards were walking away from the platform, and Brandon fell into step beside the one who had paid the conductor. "You fellows on the vigilance committee?" he said.

"No," the guard said. "We do what they tell us to do."

"Oh," Brandon said. "And who are they? Who's on the committee? Aside from Mr. Geary, that is."

The guard gave him a level look from cold eyes. "You don't know Mr. Geary's on the committee, and it ain't a good idea to think you do. The committee's the committee, and it'll see to making things right in Bigsbee, and that's all you need to know."

With Sublette dead and the north edgers gone, Brandon wondered what remained to be set right in Bigsbee, but he considered that it was not a good idea to ask the cold-eyed guard.

15

I will put another bolt in there," Ed Marks said. "It is pretty steady, but you get some jolting on those back roads, and if you put it down for good weather and up for heavy sun or rain a few times, it could work loose. Won't take above a couple of minutes."

As he worked to strengthen the supports on the new buggy top Marks said, "Looks like yesterday, bad as it was, wasn't the end of it, huh?"

"Maybe today is," Brandon said. "I just came from the station. Train pulled out with what I suppose was all the north edge on board. Looks like now there's a vigilance committee with nothing to be vigilant about."

"I hope so," Ed Marks said. "It would have been a lot better if we'd got old Jere over to Platteville and tried in the court there."

"Yeah," Brandon said. "Tried for what is hard to say, though. The worst charge, burning Harney in his place, that wouldn't stand for a second, I don't think."

"Naw," Ed Marks said, slipping a lock washer over the threaded end of a bolt protruding inside the buggy and reaching for a nut. "Art Harney fired his place like a funeral for one of them old-timey Vikings Antonelli likes to tell about and lit out, that's his way. I knowed him in the cow country, and it's what he'd do."

"I heard he rustled some out there, and Sublette was trying to use that to control him," Brandon said.

"Lots of men in Wyoming, Colorado, Utah, Texas—respected now, big men—got their start rustling," Ed Marks said. "Look back on men that has money, likely it don't take much digging to find 'em rustling, or worse, but if they get the money and use it for business and such, it don't seem to matter where it come from or how they got it. If Jere'd stolen more'n what he did and spent it on a house and a fancy rig and bought at all the stores, I expect he'd be on the town council instead of six feet under."

He stopped to look up at a tall man in the doorway of the stable. Brandon thought the new arrival might be one of the guards from the train platform but was not sure; he had the wooden, cold-eyed look, anyhow. He was, Brandon now saw, leading a lean, morose horse that looked familiar.

"You wanta buy this?" the man said.

Ed Marks shook his head. "That's Jere Sublette's horse," he said. "Rode the poor animal into the ground, Jere did, and it's no good to anyone now."

"You sell it to him?"

"Wouldn't have it in my stables *to* sell," Ed Marks said.

"Who did? You oughta know who sells horses."

"Horses, not crow bait. No idea, mister, and I doubt he'd be interested in buying it back anyways."

After the man left leading the horse, Ed Marks said, "Probably some hard-luck farmer that couldn't afford to feed the beast. But let 'em find that out for themselves. Hey, Kingslake."

Brandon turned and saw the editor and publisher of the Bigsbee *Bee* holding a stack—would you call it a swarm, Brandon wondered, or a hive?—of his papers under one arm. He looked buoyant and elated, as any

newspaperman with so salable a set of stories to print
well might.

"Not due out till tomorrow," Kingslake said, "but
with all the news, and folks in town from all around, I
figured she was worth publishing a day early. Here's
yours, Marks, with the ad on page four, as usual. Want a
copy, Blake?"

Brandon, who caught sight of the headline THE FIST OF
JUSTICE on the paper Kingslake handed to Ed Marks, did
indeed want one, and he fished the required two-cent
piece from his trousers. "I'm not usually my own news-
boy," Kingslake told Brandon. "It's for sale at the *Bee*
office, but I take the paper to the advertisers soon's it's
out, and today, with so many extra people around, I
figured it wouldn't hurt to have a few spare copies along
to sell."

"You oughta do pretty well with this one," Ed Marks
called after the departing Kingslake as he studied the
story about the Fist of Justice.

The Fist, Brandon found as he read, had clenched,
uniting the separate fingers into one powerful unit under
the pressure of disorder, depravity, and crime. It had
then raised high, lofted by the outrage of the solid
citizens of Bigsbee, and struck, wiping the slate clean of
an accumulation of crimes and criminals. Brandon
doubted that Abner Willson, proprietor of the Spargill
(Colorado) *Chronicle & Advertiser* and for a brief season
his boss, would have let a writer get away with a fist
striking and wiping in the same motion. But Kingslake
was his own boss, which often led to lax standards.

Kingslake was pretty good, Brandon considered, at
catching a striking moment or incident. The confrontation with Gannon at the door of the Seagull came across
vividly, and so did the hangdog demeanor of the north
edgers as they stood on the platform—only about an
hour before the paper went to press, Brandon realized,
unless Kingslake had been guessing ahead. As far as he
could tell, all the names mentioned were spelled right,
including his own, so Kingslake had kept the first com-

mandment of small-town newspaper publishing. The story was short, though, on some specifics, such as just who had done the actual hanging of Jere Sublette and who had arranged the expulsion of the denizens of the north edge. Wherever such a question might suggest itself, a cloud of adjective-spangled emotional and philosophical comment formed, thinning only when something more definite and comfortable appeared in the narrative.

"If I didn't know what we did yesterday, I wouldn't find out from this," Brandon said.

"That is about what you expect with the newspapers," Ed Marks said. "Anytime you are in something that happens and you read about it in the papers later on, you wonder if the reporter who got the story didn't get drunk and lose his notes and make up what he couldn't remember."

Brandon felt a little like resenting this on behalf of the self that had worked on the *Chronicle & Advertiser* and had always gotten his story straight (so far as he knew); but, remembering the unintentional travesty a couple of the St. Louis papers had made of the massacre at Mound Farm, he had to admit its justice. One had identified Elise as the sister, not the daughter, of August Ostermann; another, which had a policy critical of law enforcement agencies in general, framed its story to suggest that Elise, her father and aunt, and the workers at Mound Farm had been killed by careless firing from the posse pursuing Gren Kenneally.

"Hey, here's a little chili peppers in the stew," Ed Marks said. "Little item on page three at the end of the fist business."

Brandon turned to it.

A Job Well Done and Well Finished

The accomplishments of the Vigilance Committee, as detailed in the foregoing account, are solid and valuable to this town, and all Bigsbeans owe the

Committee appreciation. Bigsbee is a brighter place
as today's sun descends than it was at yesterday's
sunrise, with the "low-lifer" element removed from
our midst.

However, we cannot in our gratification overlook
that the rough justice administered yesterday and
today lacked legal sanctions and guarantees. While
there is no doubt that the scoundrel Sublette was
richly deserving of execution, it is a matter for
concern that no capital crime, or indeed any felony,
was actually proven against him. And there is no
doubt that, for the sake of its health, a town need not
harbor parasites any more than a human being
should, so that those who were invited to avail
themselves of a passage out of town on "the cars," at
no charge to themselves, will not be missed; yet the
overlooking of the legal formalities of expulsion and
confiscation of property, however necessary under
the circumstances obtaining, must raise a shadow of
concern.

This paper extends to the Vigilance Committee
the heartiest of congratulations on its work and
achievements, and on having fulfilled its task in so
short a time. Now that Bigsbee is cleansed of its
infective elements, the Committee has, so to speak,
worked itself out of a job, and we invite it to
disband, and its members to abandon the anonymi-
ty necessary for its function and to claim the plau-
dits of their neighbors to which they are justly
entitled.

"Interesting thinking for a newspaperman," Brandon
said. "Doesn't sound all that much like Kingslake,
somehow."

"Sound it out when you read, and you'd think you was
listening to Si Rattner speakin' at a town council meeting," Ed Marks said. "More like him than Kingslake to
take that line. If vigilantes hanged somebody every day,

Kingslake'd sell more papers than he can print. I'd say Rattner got him to put that in, prob'ly wrote it himself. There's a big ad for the bank on the back page I don't recollect seeing before, if you want to think that had anything to do with it."

"Rattner or Kingslake, it's a good thing that the vigilance committee's going to disband," Brandon said.

"Vigilantes don't like to leave off," Ed Marks said.

Brandon was not surprised, late next morning, to find Simon Rattner looking grim and haggard. The tension in the town was almost palpable from the moment he drove into it; and a glimpse of Kingslake staring out of the *Bee* office, looking a decade older and obsessed with some inward horror, was not encouraging. Brandon had planned to discuss the chances of four windmill-interested farmers getting loans, but he suspected that they would not find a place on today's agenda.

"I didn't expect it," Simon Rattner told Brandon without any preamble. "I don't know if they were so dumb they thought it was really Kingslake taking that line, or if they just figured he'd make an easier victim than me. I don't know what they did to him, but this was all over town by sunup." He tossed a smearily printed handbill at Brandon.

RETRACTION!!

The editor and publisher of the *Bee* asks his readers to forgive the intemperate expressions used toward the Vigilance Committee in yesterday's edition. We had no intention of criticizing the work of the Vigilance Committee and vigorously retract any words that might give that impression. We were unaware of many problems that require the Committee's continuing attention and withdraw our ill-considered and insulting suggestion that it disband.

We earnestly urge all Bigsbeans to cooperate with

Deathwind

the Vigilance Committee in making our town a
better place for all of us and remind them that all
who support law and order will do so, and that those
who hinder or criticize the Committee in its work
are in truth enemies of the public order.

Long live the Committee!

D. Webster Kingslake
Editor and Publisher

The type was badly aligned, and some of the letters
were reversed. Brandon could imagine frantic, trembling
fingers dropping the lead slugs into place, driven by God
knew what menace in the small hours of the morning.

Ed Marks had said it: Vigilantes don't like to leave off.
If Bigsbee didn't have any problems of crime and disorder needing their attention, problems would be found.

"Come back in a while, Blake," Simon Rattner said
wearily. "Maybe we'll be able to talk about sane things
like windmills and long-term notes then. Right now I
want to talk to Hodge and a couple of men I think I can
trust to see what we can work out about these damn
lunatics."

"Nice you feel safe talking to me that way," Brandon
said, regretting the comment when Rattner stiffened with
alarm for an instant, then relaxed.

"That's the poisonous part of this," he said. "Get these
fellows meeting in secret and masked when they're seen
and you don't know who might not be one of them.
Geary's the only one I know for sure, but I have to go
with my gut in guessing who isn't on the committee. It's
not rumbling right now, so I guess you pass." He looked
at Brandon for a moment, then said, "Maybe it's being a
salesman, but it seems to be you don't need to go
masked, Blake. I know you when I see you, and you're an
agreeable-enough-looking fellow, but somehow I'd be
hard put to say what kind of man you are. . . ." He shook
his head. "Ah, I beg your pardon, Blake, I'm woolgather-
ing. This vigilante stuff is stirring up my brains till

135

they're no better than oatmeal. Come back in about two hours, and I'll find a way to get your farmers an interest rate they can live with."

"I've been in a town when the vigilantes took over," Ed Marks said. "And it's wonderful what a bunch of law-loving men can get up to when they feel they're in the right and dealing with them that's in the wrong."

Brandon had found him sitting outside the livery stable and talking to a few other men, and he joined them. "They get fired up at robbers and killers and such, and the next thing you know, they're dealing with 'em by robbing and killing. Only it's all right, 'cause the other fellows don't deserve lawful treatment. I guess vigilantes think only innocent folks ought to get tried in a court."

Brandon considered his quest for Gren Kenneally, Farmer Dick, and the others. One of Kenneally's henchmen, guilty without a doubt, had been tried in court and acquitted, and he found justice only months later at the muzzle of Brandon's gun. He had never considered for an instant bringing any of the others to the attention of the law, though he had yet to kill any of them except in self-defense. If he had been sure Sublette was one of Gren Kenneally's gang, would he have joined in the lynching? Cole Brandon, vigilante: It had a ring he didn't like.

Flip the coin, though. The way the vigilantes were behaving, a man who had qualified to ride with Gren Kenneally could fit in with them; maybe Brandon should be looking among the committee for his man.

Shouts and excited talk swirled from up the street and came closer. Ed Marks and the group around him looked up to see two men walking rapidly along, supporting between them a third, whose feet dragged on the ground and whose bloody-faced head lolled to one side. Around them, like crows following a corn planter, men, boys, and women darted and crowded to get a glimpse and gasp and chatter about what they were seeing.

136

"Grogan!" Ed Marks called to one of the men carrying the injured man. "What happened? Who's that?"

"Peterman. Has a hay farm, what passes for a horse herd. The Vigilance Committee heard he sold Sublette that nag of his, paid him a visit last night. We found him this morning, and I hope to God the doc's in his office!"

"Why, damn!" a raw-boned man in a green canvas jacket, one of the group around Ed Marks, said loudly. "Just for selling a horse to a man that later on got hisself lynched? Those goddamn vigilantes are crazy, worse'n Jere Sublette and the north edgers boiled together in a pot!"

Some of those following the luckless Peterman and his helpers stopped and looked curiously at the speaker, as if wondering where he got his ideas . . . or, perhaps, the nerve to speak them so publicly.

With still more than three quarters of an hour to go before the time Rattner had set for his return visit, Brandon had exhausted the possibilities of coffee in Edwards's back room, talking with Carl Swanson, and buying a pair of bootlaces from Angelo Antonelli, with a free lecture on the gustatory virtues of pickled herring thrown in. He could have used a couple of shirt collars, some of his having frayed past the ability of Wen Hing to smooth them over, but he felt strongly disinclined to go anywhere near Geary's store. He walked to the eastern end of the business district of Main Street, then back partway, then over to the now-deserted station. He crossed the tracks to the riverbank and stood looking down into the water. Well into spring now, and it would be really nice to get hold of a boat and drift down it, maybe keep on drifting until you got to the Missouri, and then to the Mississippi and then on down to New Orleans and the Gulf and the open sea. You could do that, Counselor, he mused, and the world wouldn't fall apart.

He touched the coin in his pocket. It did not impart an

electric tingle to his fingers, as it had once or twice done in the past, but it felt strangely solid and real, more so than the cloth that contained it or the flesh of his thigh next to it. He could walk away from his quest; he was a free man. But he would not.

Brandon turned and walked back across the tracks and onto Main Street, surprised to see it almost clear of people for at least a block. Then he saw someone lying curled like a sick dog at the head of a side street, clutching his stomach and kicking one leg convulsively. He saw two men walking up the side street, black cloths hanging from under their hats, curtaining even the backs of their heads. A few people near enough to have the same view as Brandon were determinedly looking away from the departing vigilantes.

Brandon recognized the green canvas jacket of the man who had objected to the beating of Peterman. The vigilantes seemed to be taking to heart Kingslake's words about those who were not with them being public enemies. The beaten man managed to find his feet and walked off, those he passed contriving to keep a good distance from him.

Brandon checked his watch and decided to see if anything had come in for him at the telegraph office. No particular reason to suppose there would be, but it was something to do, and the idea of being in a place that was connected to other towns than Bigsbee, Nebraska had its attractions.

Simon Rattner and Chief Hodge seemed to have had the same idea. Brandon found them hunched over the small writing table meant for customer use.

Rattner looked up and said, "Here, Blake, take a look at this. We're doing something while there's still time, and I have the feeling that there isn't much of it."

He handed Brandon a creased sheet of paper, written in two different hands, with words crossed out and interlined so that it was abominably difficult to read, but worth the trouble.

J CAMERON SHERIFFS OFFICE PLATTEVILLE NEB. EMERGEN-
CY IN BIGSBEE REQUIRES YOUR PRESENCE AT SPECIAL MEET-
ING TOMORROW OF TOWN COUNCIL TO AVERT RIOT OR
INSURRECTION. WIRE TIME OF ARRIVAL TO UNDERSIGNED
BIGSBEE TELEGRAPH OFFICE. SIGNED T HODGE CHIEF OF
POLICE BIGSBEE AND S RATTNER PRESIDENT AGRICULTUR-
ISTS AND COMMERCIAL BANK BIGSBEE.

"Mentioning insurrection, that'll get him here on the
first train tomorrow," Rattner said. He took the paper
and handed it to the operator. "Here, Jim, you send this
out right away, and send somebody to the bank to tell me
as soon as you get a reply. And you might as well tell
anybody that comes in that the sheriff's on his way. The
faster that gets around, the faster the sand's going to leak
out of the vigilantes."

He looked back to Brandon. "Council meets in the
main room in the bank. Come on in for the meeting, and
when it's done maybe we can get to your windmills. I am
in no frame of mind to deal with them now."

16

I now call this council into session," Simon Rattner said.

"How can you do that, Rattner?" one of the six councilmen said. "You ain't even *on* the council."

"I am a citizen, property owner, and taxpayer of Bigsbee, Nebraska," Simon Rattner said. "And as such I am exercising my right to call for a special meeting of the town council as the bylaws specify can be done in case of emergency."

There was no such provision, Rattner had told Brandon as they waited for the train bringing Sheriff Cameron to Bigsbee that morning, "but there's enough bylaws nobody can understand so they can't be sure of it. It's wonderful what a tangle lawyers can make of things even when they're not trying to."

"Are they ever not trying?" Brandon said. It was a long time since he had practiced law, and he found it hard to believe that he had spent hours in wrapping a simple circumstance in strand after strand of cobwebby precedent so that it would be unassailable in court and unintelligible elsewhere.

Now, in the crowded front room of the bank, the six councilmen sat behind a table against one wall, facing about thirty townsmen who had pushed in and were sitting on a few benches or standing or lounging against the walls. Sheriff Cameron, a blockily built man with a flat red face that gave him a look of perpetual anger, sat in a padded armchair that Rattner had pulled out from his office. He was flanked by two hard-faced men in dark suits, the jackets of which were eased back to display holstered revolvers; deputies and bodyguards, Brandon supposed.

"We're here because Jim Cameron wanted us here, and not because of any nonsense about you calling us into session, Si," said Danby the barber, the only one of the councilmen Brandon knew. He turned to where the sheriff sat and said, "We're here and open for business, Jim. Now you tell us why."

"The emergency and disorder in your town, Danby," the sheriff said.

"There was some excitement a couple days ago," Danby said. "Unfortunate death of one Sublette whilst resisting arrest, the which our chief of police, Ted Hodge, didn't seem to feel called for charges being brought. That right, Ted?"

Hodge, standing in one corner, nodded. Well, no, Brandon thought. The head of a two-man police force is not going to get involved in arresting a good part of the town that hires him; one thing about a mob is the distribution of guilt—all over everyone, but spread thin.

"And this Sublette being the chiefest example of wrongdoing hereabouts, with him gone, a lot of folks that had the bad judgment to look up to him, why, they got discouraged and left town, so there's nobody left to give cause for any emergencies and disorders," Danby said, smooth as his own razor gliding across a customer's underjaw and removing obstructive bristles.

"The Vigilance Committee," the sheriff said.

"There was talk of that," Danby said. "I heard it, the other men on the council heard it. Masked men beating and threatening people and such. But we haven't seen it, that's the thing, Jim. No fellows with black handkerchiefs over their faces doing any of those kinds of things. I ask you, members of the town council, any of you see anything like that?"

The five other councilmen shook their heads, said "No," "Not me," "Nope," "Naw," and a second plain "No." Brandon wondered who they were and supposed they had to be businessmen whose services he had not had occasion to use: feed merchant, undertaker, land office, and the like. The tall one with the long nose and lank black hair could be the undertaker; easy to see him standing like a vulture at the graveside—he had even given his negative answer to Danby's question in a kind of grating croak. The short one, called "Toad" if there were any justice to nicknames, Brandon could not assign an occupation to. He suspected that Bigsbee's town council, as often happened, was mainly composed of men with undemanding and consequently unrewarding businesses who fell into public office as a means of acquiring some standing, finding it easy to do so because nobody else wanted the job. The exception was Danby, who was busy, widely known, and well enough liked, and therefore had the effective power to run the council about as he liked. There wasn't much for the town council of a place like Bigsbee to do, but what there was, Danby was ready to do, making little secret of looking on the others as not much more than clothing-store dummies: good window dressing, but not expected to take any action.

"If you fellows haven't seen anything, others have," Simon Rattner said. "There was old man Peterman that had to be taken to the doctor's—he was beaten up by the Vigilance Committee. And after that, right on Main Street, they attacked someone they didn't like."

"What's Peterman have to say about what happened to him?" Danby said.

"He wouldn't come to the meeting," Simon Rattner said. "Too scared."

"And the other man, the one on Main Street? Did witnesses see the Vigilance Committee doing anything to him?"

"Ah . . ." Simon Rattner looked around the room. At least three people Brandon had seen near the scene of the beating looked blankly back at him. Rattner's gaze settled on Brandon. "Mr. Calvin Blake, a temporary resident, was an eyewitness to that."

Brandon damned Rattner silently and rose. Neither his work for Nonpareil nor his pursuit of Gren Kenneally's satellite would be helped by getting involved in this, but there was no help for it now.

He answered Danby's question about what he had seen, and Danby said, "What it amounts to, someone down and two men with their faces hidden going away from him. You see these men actually with him, hurting him?"

Brandon said he had not. "Okay," Danby said, "though I admit it looks as if they did it. But if you're going after somebody you don't like on Main Street in the middle of the afternoon, it makes sense to hide your face so nobody can't go to Ted Hodge and tell him who to lock up. Everybody's got some enemies, and who's to say this fellow didn't, and that they didn't catch up with him? Come down to it, there's only hearsay and speculation that there's a Vigilance Committee at all."

"Crap," Sheriff Cameron said. "You had yourselves a lynching, and you had yourselves a goddamn Vigilance Committee, like some damn fool mining town in California, and the vigilantes did what vigilantes do. They figure they're better at running the place than anybody else, and they try to take over. Well, gentlemen of the town council, I will tell you in my book that's civil disorder, sedition, and insurrection."

He stared at the town council, at Simon Rattner, at the audience occupying most of the room, and at several people peering in from the street. "Now, I have had some experience with insurrections, as some of you know. There was the Copley County War over in Wyoming, for one." Brandon remembered vaguely some story of a rivalry between ranchers that had grown explosively, like a giant boil, and then been brutally lanced by decisive action by the authorities under the direction of one Campbell—or maybe, now he thought of it, Cameron. . . .

"Insurrection, disorder, and sedition is *almost* the worst thing that can happen to a place," Cameron went on. "The worst thing is what gets done to a place in putting down sedition and disorder and insurrection. The way I do it, anyhow."

Danby's jaunty, contemptuous manner had faded by the time Cameron finished. Simon Rattner was looking at the sheriff with a touch of unease.

"What I want now is the council's assurance that this Vigilance Committee is, as from this moment, out of business," Cameron said.

"But," Danby said, "it ain't even established that there is, or that there was, any Vigilance Committee."

"Crap again," Cameron said. "But if that was to be so, then there'd be no problem about giving the assurance, would there? Either way, I want the town council's word that I don't hear nothing more about the vigilantes or other insurrections here in Bigsbee. You just pass yourselves an ordinance dissolving any vigilante organizations there might happen to be and forbidding any such in the future, and it's settled. And you better mean it, for if I have to come back, I won't be alone, and Copley County'll be spoke of like a Methodist social beside Bigsbee."

Danby and even Rattner seemed to be struggling with the impulse to tell Cameron that he could not threaten them like that, but apparently they decided that in fact he could and kept silent on the point. "Si," Danby said, "you want to help me out with the words on this?"

The resolution Danby and Rattner prepared stipulated that all actions in enforcement of law and order were strictly reserved to the town's police force or to individuals deputized by them; that the wearing of masks or other disguises, or the concealment of identity by other means —you're breaking the law even as they make it, Counsel-

or, Brandon told himself with a touch of amusement—
was prohibited; and that all intimidation or attempts to
influence actions by threats were also prohibited.

"This is an emergency ordinance," Danby told the
crowd, "and when things ease off we'll cut back on her
so's a fistfight or a costume in the Fourth of July parade
ain't unlawful." He cast a sour glance at Cameron as he
spoke but did not seem inclined to take his irritation at
the sheriff's interference further.

"I now put this motion to the council," Danby said.
"Second?"

The man Brandon thought of as Toad opened his
mouth broadly enough to snap up a fly and seconded the
motion. "Favor, opposed, motion carried," Danby said
without bothering to look at the council members as they
indicated their assent. The audience obliged with moderate applause.

Danby adjourned the council meeting, Rattner escorted Sheriff Cameron to the station, and the crowd
began to disperse.

Brandon had expected to see Kingslake at the meeting,
gathering news for the *Bee*, and Geary, whose outspoken
advocacy of vigilante action had spurred the expedition
after Sublette and whose stock had furnished the committee's masks; but neither was in the room or, as far as
he could see, in the crowd outside.

Whether word of Swicegood's satisfaction with his
windmill had traveled, or the town council's resolution
promoted a general optimism about the future, or from
some other cause entirely, Brandon had sold two Nonpareils by the afternoon of the next day. The second was to
a farmer east and a touch north of town, and Brandon's
route to the post office to mail the orders in—only the
first sale had merited the special treatment of
telegraphing—took him through the now-deserted north
edge. He saw the abandoned hulk of the Seagull a little
distance to his right, with the paneless window Jere

Sublette had gone through open like a toothless mouth. He thought the wooden bird over the front door was a little askew but could not be sure at this distance and had no intention of going nearer.

The north edge wasn't entirely deserted, though; as he passed one of the shacks a man's face peered boldly out. He didn't seem concerned about being seen but followed Brandon with his gaze as the buggy rolled by. There was the faintest touch of familiarity about the face, and after a moment Brandon thought he placed it among those who, only a few days before, had stood on the train platform waiting to be carried into permanent exile from Bigsbee.

In the post office two men who seemed to have no mailing to do stood idly around, studying the wanted posters and postal notices on the walls or apparently admiring the ornately decorated lock boxes. Brandon found a place at the splinter-surfaced writing counter, scraped a deposit of dried ink off the post office's pen, dipped it in the inkwell, and addressed the order envelope to Nonpareil in Chicago, cramped a little by the man who moved to stand next to him and execute an intricate design on the blotter with his thumbnail.

"This isn't goddamn going to *do!*" Simon Rattner said. He slammed his fist on his desk, sending the papers and ledgers into an upward flinch. Brandon wondered if he would ever get to talk to Rattner about getting his customers loans without something coming up to interfere.

"What won't do?"

"It's still going on! Last night a man was dragged from his house and kicked and beaten by men with masks, told it was because he bad-mouthed the Vigilance Committee, and I just now got word that one of the men that complained to me about the Vigilance Committee before I called Sheriff Cameron in was found tied up in the stable back of his house, his mouth jammed open and a clothespin pegged to his tongue. It's as if the town council never passed that resolution."

"You ask Geary about this?" Brandon said. "They say it's his stock the vigilantes used for masks."

Simon Rattner nodded wearily. "Says he's got nothing to do with it, he's shocked, black cloth can come from anywheres, was in his store doing inventory when things happened, and on and on. Maybe he's even telling the truth. I don't think there's anything to do now but call Cameron back, which I hate to. There is a line in some poem or play that goes, 'Cry Havoc! and let slip the dogs of war.' Once I wire Cameron, that's havoc, all right: He'll get things settled, but there'll be burying to do after, I'm afraid. Come on along and help me fire on Fort Sumter."

Like the post office the day before, the telegraph office harbored a seeming noncustomer, a man Brandon thought he recognized as one of those who had guarded the north edgers on the station platform. He was not wearing a gun belt, but the bulge of a pocketed revolver was clearly visible as he lounged against the counter containing the message forms. He stared hard at Rattner as he came in, and Brandon saw the telegraph operator look from one to the other with a trapped rabbit's desperation.

He stepped forward and said, "What's the line condition today?"

"Ah, to . . ." the operator said huskily.

Brandon pitched his voice low enough not to carry to the man leaning on the counter. "Platteville."

"Ah . . . break in that line, I'm afraid," the operator gabbled, as if each destination the telegraph linked to Bigsbee had its own circuit.

Brandon stepped back and rejoined Simon Rattner, took him by the arm, and turned him toward the door. "Line's down," he said loudly. "Can't wire Fidelity in Omaha about the debentures." To his relief, Rattner was a quick thinker and did not resist being urged out of the office, nor did he demand to know what Brandon was doing, prating of debentures. In the street he said, "They're blocking the telegraph?"

Brandon nodded. "Got the clerk buffaloed. The jasper with the gun'll see who tries to send anything. For certain he'll see any messages before they're sent. I think they've got people at the post office checking who's writing where, too."

Rattner did not argue that Brandon was exaggerating or complain about the suddenly growing menace. He pulled his watch from his vest and said, "We'll do it direct, then. Eastbound train's in ten minutes. We'll go on to Platteville and tell Cameron in person how things are."

Brandon looked across to the station platform. "Maybe. If those fellows standing around are passengers, anyhow. I kind of don't think they are."

Simon Rattner studied the three men on the platform. "Cut from the same bolt as the one in the telegraph office, no question. I could buy a ticket to Omaha, not Platteville, though."

"I don't think," Brandon said, "that you or anybody else they think is against them is going to be taking the train anywhere for a while."

"But damn it," Rattner said, "they can't cut a whole town off from the world like that!"

"If they control what goes out of the post office or on the telegraph and who goes on the train, they can do a pretty good job of cutting us off, at least for a while," Brandon said. "May be one way around it, though."

"Saddle horses ain't my favorite," Ed Marks said, "but I do keep a few, since the customers want 'em, and these are pretty good."

"They'll do for us," Brandon said. He had decided against using the buggy—horses were more flexible and drew less attention—and would leave it at Marks's stable. "You know the road to Platteville?"

"Faster and cheaper to take the train," Ed Marks said.

"Not today."

"Suit yourselves. Anyhow, if you follow on east past Swicegood's, that's it. Farm roads off it from time to time. Twenty miles or so on, it goes down by the river for a ways, around a kind of hill that's pretty high for these parts, and once you get past that you're about halfway."

As Brandon had figured, there were no sentinels at the edge of town; too much traffic to and from farms to make checking movements by horse or wagon practical. He and Rattner passed the territory he knew, and he pointed out Swicegood's Kickapoo Sagwa-embellished windmill with a proprietary pride before passing on into unfamiliar countryside. This was pretty much identical to what came before it, though now it was open prairie rather than cultivated farmland.

"I think we're doing this just about in time," Brandon said. "They haven't had time to box everything up, but in a day or so they'd work out how to. When it's all sorted out I expect you'll find one of the vigilantes had some experience taking and holding towns during the war."

"When it's all sorted out what I mainly want to find out is who the hell is behind it and what the hell they're up to," Simon Rattner said. "I am all for boosting Bigsbee, and if there was going to be a Bigsbee pavilion at the Centennial Exposition I would contribute heavily to the building fund, but I have to say that there ain't much about the place to make it worth taking over. Bigsbee is the kind of place that gets those ciphers on the town council as its elders and governors, and even they are good enough for what Bigsbee needs most times, with Danby telling them what to do. What're the damn vigilantes after?"

Brandon interpreted Rattner's talk as complaint rather than the opening of a discussion and kept silent. For some men, exercise of power was an end in itself; they beat and terrorized to beat and terrorize, not to gain an end. Usually they managed to find some profit in the situation all the same. From what he had heard, Gren

Kenneally would have brutalized and murdered even apart from his robberies, but the loot made him a criminal, not a plain lunatic.

He realized now that what had made him join Rattner in an enterprise that was none of his business was an awareness that one of Gren Kenneally's men was somewhere hereabouts, probably the Farmer Dick the report had mentioned. It was like a faint star seen from the corner of the eye but not straight on; he had not felt the awareness directly, but, looking back, he could sense that it had been there fleetingly during the last few days. The notion he had had, talking outside Ed Marks's place just before the beaten Peterman had been hustled along to the doctor, that the vigilantes included men worthy of association with Gren Kenneally was worth following up, as he was now doing.

He also realized that one possible answer to Rattner's question was simple and evident. Bigsbee didn't have much, but one of the things it did have was a bank. Once the vigilantes controlled the town, there would be no way of defending the bank from them.

Slowly, like waves rising on the ocean but two hundred times slower, the land rose around them, peaking into low hills and crests, and the track angled down, following the river, which had deserted the distant railroad tracks and wandered northward for a while. A dome-shaped hill with a copse of trees on the top loomed ahead and, though not more than fifty feet higher than the ground it rose from, dominated the prospect as much as a prominence ten times its height would have in less flat country.

Brandon was wondering if the Indians who had yielded this land to the encroaching settlers had used the hill as an outpost when he received a demonstration that it was at least a possibility. A puff of smoke formed among the trees, and he heard the slap of a shot and saw dirt spout from the trail twenty feet ahead.

He and Simon Rattner reined up. Brandon saw that the trail ahead provided no cover and recalled that the top of the hill had been in their view for some time, so that there was no shelter immediately behind them, either. The distance by which the shot had missed, and the fact that it had not been followed by others, indicated that it was a warning to go no further.

"Back to Bigsbee, I guess," Rattner said. "They moved faster than I thought."

Brandon was not dismayed at not getting through to Platteville. If whatever was moving the pieces around the board in this game he had been living since St. Louis set him back in Bigsbee, then so be it. A tough thread of certainty in his gut told him that his quarry was in Bigsbee, and finding him was what mattered, not whether some crazed vigilantes wrecked the town.

17

This is excellent, Miss Helen, and I'm grateful to you for inviting me," Simon Rattner said.

There was easily enough of the flavorful main dish—ham, potatoes, and onions baked together with some milk; Brandon found that his term as a trail cook had left him with an analytical approach toward what he was served—to suggest that it had been prepared with left-over servings in mind, so that when Brandon and Rattner turned up at dusk on their way back from the interrupted journey to Platteville it had not much disarranged Helen Kitson's domestic economy to insist they share supper.

Brandon had made the slight detour only to let his hosts know he would be turning up well after dark, after returning the saddle horse to Ed Marks and retrieving the buggy, but was glad of the invitation. It had been a long day, with nothing to eat since breakfast. Simon Rattner, facing the dark ride back to Bigsbee and what late meal his hired woman felt like giving him, also welcomed it.

Walter Kitson appeared impressed by having the banker as his guest and was fascinated by his account of the attempt to reach Sheriff Cameron. "D'you have to go by that road?" he asked. "Lots of open country. Couldn't you sort of circle around, come into Platteville from another direction?"

"Likely," Brandon said. "But that hill commands a far view, and you'd have to go a pretty long way around not to be seen. And if the vigilantes have someone posted there, they could be other places as well. You'd have to get up at least a small party to have a good chance of getting through, and that would take some organizing."

"It might be better if we could find out who the Vigilance Committee is," Simon Rattner said. "Daytimes they'll be at their work, like everybody else, and if we knew who they were, Chief Hodge and some trustworthy men could take them in one at a time, and the whole business would collapse. The men who're doing their bidding wouldn't have anybody to take orders from. That way, it'd be handled without calling in the sheriff, which is likely to be bloody."

Walter Kitson shook his head. "I am for law and orderliness and righteous doings, and it's a puzzlement to me that whichever way you go at it, it seems to come to violence and schemings. That Sublette was an offense in the sight of the Lord, but hanging him out of hand, that's wrongdoing, too. And the harlots and publicans and sinners from the north edge, they deserve being cast out into the darkness, but it was done the wrong way." Brandon remembered the face he had seen in the supposedly deserted north edge—and now, come to think of it, one of the men in the post office—and wondered just how effective the casting-out had been.

"And now you and Mr. Blake, to get what's lawful done, you've got to sneak out of town and get shot at, like outlaws working up a raid," Walter Kitson said gloomily. "I was brought up to do right and to expect other folks to do right, and if you done that, things would go right for you. You reap what you sow."

He inspected a forkful of potato before consuming it, chewed a moment, and said, "It works in farming, some.

You plant seed potatoes, and what comes up is a potato. But then it might not come up at all, or the drought or the hoppers get it, or the railroad takes away all the profit, and none of that don't have to do with how you walk in the ways of the Lord or you don't. And you get together with other farmers in the Grange to see what you can do about it, and now that don't work neither!" He looked savagely at his plate and dug into the food as if he were more intent on destroying than enjoying it.

"There was to be a Grange meeting in Bigsbee tonight," Helen Kitson said, "and Walter was looking forward to it. But they sent word this afternoon that the meeting was called off. Boy that brought the message wasn't sure why, something about safety."

"Could be the Grange people don't know what the vigilantes will get up to," Brandon said.

"Or the vigilantes decided they didn't want a large crowd getting together that might decide to fight 'em," Simon Rattner said.

"It's a hard thing to be against folks that claim to be for decency and uprightness, and against lewdness and sin," Walter Kitson said. Brandon saw that Helen Kitson's face registered only respectful interest but saw vividly in recollection her happily wanton expression and the proud curve of her body in the photograph; he suspected Walter Kitson would consider it a perfect representation of lewdness and sin.

"I don't know of anybody that claims to be *for* lewdness and sin," Simon Rattner said. Brandon tried to think of a town he had been in that did not have establishments or whole sections advertising and promoting every variety of vice, from the lavish brothels of San Francisco to the hells-on-wheels that sprang up at the head of construction on the railroads. But whores and gamblers and con men were more honest about their aims than vigilantes usually were, so Rattner was right in spirit, if not in actuality.

Rich apple pie and strong coffee lightened the mood, and Walter Kitson and Simon Rattner began a courtly conversational dance around the topic of windmills and how to finance them. As far as Brandon could tell, the object of the ritual was to see whether Rattner would offer a loan or Kitson would ask for one.

"I believe in keeping my machinery in good repair," Walter Kitson said. "That way I can be sure of harvesting what I grow, even with more water. Come on out to the barn and I'll show you."

He took a lantern and led Rattner out of the kitchen.

Helen Kitson filled Brandon's coffee cup, sat down opposite him, and waited for nearly a minute after the door closed behind her nephew and his guest before speaking.

"You're taking the horse you hired back tonight?" she said.

"I was. Now I'm here, thought I'd stay, go to Bigsbee in the morning."

"Would you go tonight?" Helen Kitson said.

Brandon stirred his coffee. Helen Kitson knew as well as he the extent—not all that great—of the inconvenience she was asking of him; therefore she had a good reason for asking, and therefore he would do it. "Sure, if you want."

"Thank you," she said. "I was going in myself, to see my friend—"

"Swanson," Brandon said. At this point, and with the image of her photographs still in his mind, her reticence seemed pointless.

She glanced at the door, then back at Brandon. "Yes. I was going to go to Carl's place. He lives behind his store. I'd leave a little after Walter and be sure to come back before he finished his Grange meeting. It's not that much time, but . . ." Worth the trip, Brandon finished silently, seeing the mingled longing and sensuality that softened her face.

"And now the meeting's off, and Walter's here for the evening, and so are you," Brandon said. "Okay, I'll go in to town and let him know you can't meet him tonight."

"And tell him I'll find a way to tell him when we'll get together next," Helen Kitson said softly.

Whenever it is, he'll be a lucky man, Brandon thought.

"You can tell Marks I'll be along in a few minutes," Brandon said. "I want to drop in on Swanson, talk to him about the advertising signs for the windmills."

"I don't see any lights in the store," Simon Rattner said.

"He'll be in his quarters around back," Brandon said.

Rattner's horse moved off toward Ed Marks's stable, first indistinct, then invisible in the unlit street.

Brandon found the alley beside Carl Swanson's shop and nudged his horse into it. There were no lights visible in the back of the building either. Naturally, Brandon thought, he wouldn't want to light up his lady-love creeping across the yard. Guess he hasn't given up on her yet, then, even though it's late. He'll be disappointed it's me.

Brandon tapped on the back door and, to forestall any embarrassingly sudden greeting, said, "Swanson—it's me, Blake, Calvin Blake. Got to talk to you."

There was no answer, and he rapped louder. A faint noise from inside the darkened building sounded like a voice, and it could have been saying "Come in," as much as anything. Brandon tried the latch, and the door eased open. He caught his breath as an acrid chemical smell stung his throat, nose, and eyes.

He heard the voicelike noise again, something between a groan and a muttered attempt at speech. He stepped carefully into the room, his shoes crunching on what felt and sounded like fragments of glass underfoot.

Brandon stopped, fished a match from his pocket, and struck it on his thumbnail. Scattered splinters of light winked from the floor, and a larger, flickering reflection shone from the glass chimney of a lantern on a table in front of him. He opened it and held the match to the wick, touching it into light just before the match burned his fingers.

He held up the lantern, and its light washed across the room. It was small, not much more than ten feet on a side, and simply furnished, with two chairs, a table, and a low bed. A figure was draped on the edge of the bed, head and shoulders on the mattress, knees on the floor.

"Plague," a voice said thickly. After a moment of shock Brandon translated this as an attempt at "Blake" and went over to the bed. Carl Swanson's head was turned to one side, and he rolled an eye to stare up at Brandon. "Fidge landies," he muttered through puffed lips.

"Vigilantes did this to you?"

"Hnyah. Boud nour hgo. Was wadin' . . ."

Swanson had been waiting in his room for a friend to visit him, he told Brandon, and answered a knock at the back door. Instead of the friend there had been three men with black cloths covering their faces. They stepped inside the room, and one of them flourished an envelope at him, addressed The Sheriff's Office, Platteville, Nebr.

"Asked me if I'd written it," Swanson said, speaking more easily now as he got used to moving his bruised lips. "They knew I did, 'cause the envelope was opened, and they had the letter I wrote Cameron telling him how things were going here. Didn't wait for an answer but knocked me down with some kind of club and commenced to kicking me. One of 'em rummaged around in the next room and come out with some plates I'd just made and smashed 'em over my head. Guess he knocked over a bottle of acid I use for developing, from the smell."

Brandon considered Swanson's news with some dismay. The watchers in the post office might have seen the address on the letter Swanson handed in, as they presumably had when he had sent his orders in to Nonpareil in Chicago, an innocuous destination. But having the letter itself argued that the vigilantes had access to the privacies of the post office, either by intimidating the postmaster or because he was one of them.

Swanson hawked and spat. "They showed me the

letter, tore it up, and made me eat it, and when I'd done that they hit me some more, till I passed out. Hey, what time is it? My friend . . ."

"She won't be coming tonight," Brandon said. "Asked me to come tell you, that's why I'm here. Walter's Grange meeting got called off."

"Oh. She, uh, she told you . . ."

"That you have an understanding," Brandon said. "Walter'd get upset if he knew, so that's why you have to be quiet about it, she told me that."

"She's a good woman, Blake," Carl Swanson said. "Wasn't for Walter feeling so, I'd be proud to have it known I was courting her." His eyes suddenly moved to focus on the next room and widened. Brandon suspected he had been reminded of just how good a woman Helen Kitson was, and the photographs he had to prove it.

"Better see if those fellows did any more damage or stole any stuff," he said, and he limped into the workroom. Brandon did not follow. In a moment Swanson returned carrying a tied-up stack of prints that Brandon recognized, having done the typing up himself. "Family pictures," Swanson said, dropping the bundle on his bed. "Hate to have lost them."

"You can't replace memories," Brandon said. "Anything else torn up or gone?"

"No," Carl Swanson said. "Not yet."

Brandon nodded. The vigilantes might expect that Carl Swanson would be terrified into submission and passivity, but it was going to occur to them soon enough that they had no guarantee of that, and that it would be best to take no chances with him. With people like that, suspicion, fear, and violence fed on one another, intensifying into further brutality. They would be back, almost certainly.

"You've got to get away," he said. "My buggy's at Ed Marks's. I'll get it and come back here, take you . . ." He paused.

"Where?"

"The Kitsons'," Brandon said after a moment. "Far enough away, and the vigilantes won't think to come looking for you there. You can stay in the barn to be extra sure, in case they do come out for a look around."

"They won't, uh . . ."

"Walter distrusts the vigilantes, and my guess is he'll want to help someone who's fallen foul of them." Brandon paused and looked at Swanson's battered face. "Somehow I don't think Helen will mind any extra trouble you'll make."

Brandon decided that he could take a chance with Ed Marks; the liveryman's loathing of the vigilantes was almost palpable and could not—he hoped—be assumed, especially as Brandon could see nothing to be gained by such dissimulation. He explained Swanson's situation and added, "We'd best get what we can of his stuff out of his store along with him. If that crowd comes back and finds him gone, they'll destroy what's there, and he'll be left with his life but no way to make a living."

"We'll load the buggy with all it'll take," Ed Marks said. "Camera, his important pictures, and so on, the stuff he can't afford to lose. I'll get a dray over there and clean out everything else before dawn, hide it in the stable. With luck, nobody'll see anything, and the bastards won't know what happened. Maybe they'll beshit themselves, wondering if Swanson found a way to get through to Platteville. That'd be nice. Swanson I don't care much about one way or another, but whatever I can do that makes the world a meaner place for them vigilantes, that'll make me feel good all over."

Marks looked at the saddle horse Brandon had just returned. "You know," he said, "why don't you keep the nag for a while? Way things are going, you never know when you're going to have to move fast and light, and there's times when you're just not going to want the buggy. Tie him on behind it and lead him out to the farm, and he'll be handy if you need him. There's times a good horse is all that's between you and something awful bad behind you."

It was Ed Marks's thought to tack blankets over the street-side windows to shut off the lantern light as they stripped Swanson's shop. Camera equipment, developing material, Swanson's photographs of the West, and his business records went into the buggy, barely leaving room for Swanson himself. Furniture, painting material, the huge stencils Swanson had cut for application of advertisements to the windmill vanes, and anything else went into the dray.

"You get on the way," Ed Marks said. "I'll have this loaded in not much longer, and it'll be stowed safe away in my place before sunrise."

"Thanks," Brandon said, and he climbed up onto the buggy's seat. He looked behind him, squinting, and made out Swanson's blanket-wrapped form lying among his effects. He touched the whip to the horse, and the buggy moved ahead, sluggish and squashy on its springs from the extra weight. He wondered if there were a way to persuade the saddle horse tied behind to push a little.

A rap on the side of the buggy stopped him. Ed Marks held up a twine-tied bundle. "Started to take the bed— this was on it."

Brandon said "Thanks" again, took the photographs, and set them on the empty seat next to him, then realized they might slide off and tucked them into the fabric pocket attached to the buggy's inside panel.

Well, now, Counselor, he thought, you are saving Swanson's bacon, throwing him together with his inamorata, joining forces with a liveryman and a banker to frustrate the malice of a bunch of vigilantes, and also doing a nice sideline in selling windmills. You better hope some of that ties in to hunting that sidekick of Gren's that's supposed to be here, or it's all a waste of time.

18

Brandon gaped at Helen Kitson like an idiot. She did look fetching, face still a little swollen and flushed with sleep, wearing a voluminous wrapper against the morning chill; however, Brandon was not openmouthed in response to her appearance, but as a result of the massive yawn that had seized him. It was well after one in the morning when he settled Carl Swanson into the barn, still blanket-wrapped in the buggy, the most comfortable accommodation immediately available, and it was now somewhat after half-past five. The hours between had not afforded much sleep, as Brandon knew he had to talk to Helen Kitson before Walter appeared in the kitchen for his pre-chore coffee, and to talk to Walter before he went to the barn and found it contained a tenant who had not been there the night before. Each time he allowed himself to doze, reminding himself sternly that he must not sleep past five, he came awake, checked his pocket watch, and found that his slumber had lasted ten to twenty-five minutes.

He watched hungrily while Helen Kitson set the coffee-pot on the stove and stirred and refueled the fire that had been banked overnight. "He's not hurt, just bruised some," he told her. "I left him wrapped up in a blanket in the buggy, sleeping peaceful, and I put the camera and pictures and stuff up in the loft so he's got room. It's as comfortable as a bed, almost."

Helen Kitson took a deep breath. "I know I can't go out to him yet, but it's a comfort to know you took care of him. I . . . Walter's coming."

Walter Kitson came into the kitchen and looked at Brandon with surprise.

"I'm up early because I've got something to tell you and Miss Helen," Brandon said. He explained what he had found at Carl Swanson's shop the night before and why he had thought it best to spirit Swanson and his effects away. Walter Kitson looked astonished and alarmed; Brandon's early disclosure to Helen Kitson allowed her to assume an expression of concern suitable to hearing of the misfortunes of a tradesman whose services she had employed.

"It was a liberty, I know," Brandon said. "But this was the safest place I could think of. I know it'll mean extra work for Miss Helen, and there could be danger if the vigilantes get word he's here. If you want me to try to find another place—"

"An extra meal or so's no bother on a farm," Helen Kitson said briskly. "And from what you say, there's no reason for anyone to think Mr. Swanson's here, and if he keeps to the barn during daylight, nobody'd ever see him."

"Ah," Walter Kitson said, "I guess I can do it. To beat a man because he sent a letter, that's wrong. And Swanson's a good enough fellow far's I know. Did a good job on that picture of Father, too, and I was thinking he might do one of Helen, take her picture and crayon it in, like for Father."

Brandon's gaze flicked involuntarily to Helen Kitson's face. When their eyes met, hers widened in instant understanding, then narrowed as a brief grin flashed. She doesn't seem to mind I've seen what she looks like without a stitch, Brandon thought; hope she doesn't think Swanson showed them to me, though.

"Best let Mr. Swanson sleep while you're in the barn, Walter," Helen Kitson said. "I'll see to whatever he might need while you're out in the fields."

Walter Kitson nodded, finished his coffee, and left the kitchen for the chill dawn outside. Brandon had the fancy that if Walter looked back he would see the windows aglow with the radiance of his aunt's smile.

Brandon stirred his coffee and hoped that Carl Swanson and Helen Kitson could maintain celibacy during Swanson's stay. He abandoned the thought as soon as it was formed as completely unrealistic, substituting a hope for enough discretion to avoid arousing Walter Kitson's passions against the livelier sins.

Brandon made up some of his arrears of sleep during the morning but found himself unable to keep to his bed much after eleven, and he settled in the kitchen to do some paperwork for Nonpareil. He had supposed that writing an order to go to the home office and writing a payment receipt to go to the customer was all that was required, but modern business seemed almost as bad as the law for obliging a man to deface bits of paper. He found that he had fallen behind on his sales diary, and that he now had to prepare customer evaluations without the benefit of the notes he should have taken while on the call.

It is fortunate that a stretch in journalism developed your talent for fiction, Counselor, he thought, and he began fulfilling Ralph Catesby's injunctions as best he could, aiming for plausibility rather than pedantic accuracy. Simon Rattner also needed some information for loans under consideration, but Brandon had taken care to gather the needed facts, so that was little trouble.

As he worked Helen Kitson would come in, perform some tasks, and go out, mentioning that Mr. Swanson in the barn might be glad of a snack or a drink or a book to read. At each entrance she was more radiant than before, until she seemed to glow through her clothing. Brandon inferred that Carl Swanson had recovered remarkably from his beating and was not much distressed by his sudden exile from home and business; he hoped the couple would not occasion spontaneous combustion in the hayloft.

About midafternoon he decided his paperwork was as done as it was going to be, and that he had what he needed for Rattner and might as well take it in to Bigsbee. He considered going up to his room and retrieving his .38 but decided not to. With things as edgy in Bigsbee as they were now, the best thing would be to avoid situations where guns might come into play.

In the barn he found Carl Swanson lying on a pad of blankets and reading a book. "Helen gave me this to read to pass the time," he said.

"Poetry? Practical farming?" Brandon said.

"Naw, story book. About a girl that falls down a rabbit hole."

"And then she gets rescued by Fred Fearnot or such just before the prairie fire gets to her?"

"Not quite," Carl Swanson said. "You going to town?"

Brandon nodded. "I'll take the saddle horse in, though, not the buggy; you might as well stay in it."

"Yeah," Carl Swanson said. "It's comfortable, and real well sprung. You'll take a look at what's happened to my place?"

"Sure," Brandon said. "Every time I go to Bigsbee there's something strange going on. I wonder what it'll be like today."

"Curiouser and curiouser, I expect," Carl Swanson said.

The sign was gone from in front of Carl Swanson's store, and a plank was nailed across the front door. Ed Marks had contrived to make the place look as if it had been deserted a month ago. Brandon thought it significant that there was not a knot of curious people standing around the abandoned building discussing what might have happened. Bigsbeans seemed to have learned to suppress curiosity in these last few days.

"Marks told me about it," Simon Rattner said after Brandon had started his account of Carl Swanson's misadventures. "If Swanson stays out of sight, maybe it'll get them to do something foolish. I hope that happens soon, if it's going to, for things don't look good. There's men around town now that were driven out with the north edgers, and the only thing that can mean is that the vigilantes got to them and are using them. There is something almighty bad building up."

"Have you thought that they might be after the bank? Wait until they feel strong enough with those north edgers and all, to just come in and take out what you've got?"

"It's a possibility," Simon Rattner said. "I've been talking to some men I think I know I can trust, and we might be able to stop that, but it'd be a pure horror if we set up another Vigilance Committee to fight the first one—bad as having the War back again. I haven't been able to get a clue about who the vigilantes are, except for Geary, and he doesn't seem to go near anyone else. Keep your eyes open, Blake, and let me know if you see anything. Now, you have those papers? Let's see if we can make some loans to your customers while there's still money in the bank."

Brandon decided to delay his return to the Kitson farm until just before supper. He did not care to spend the latter part of the afternoon sitting in the kitchen or parlor, watching Helen Kitson going to or coming from Carl Swanson and wondering if Walter Kitson would return from the fields unexpectedly early to find his aunt flagrantly delicting with his new guest.

He had left his horse at Ed Marks's stable on coming in to town and now walked from the bank along Main Street, past the railroad station. The platform was deserted; no train was due for the rest of the day, so there was no reason for the vigilantes' henchmen to intimidate prospective passengers. Brandon saw the river glinting in the late afternoon sun and walked across the tracks to it.

The bank was steeply cut, but no more than six feet high. Brandon scrambled down it to the narrow strip of pebbles that bordered the water, and he was cut off from the town. He felt a sharp sense of relief and realized how oppressive the atmosphere in Bigsbee had become. It was a slight compensation to think that a place that troubled was the most likely kind of hunting ground for the game he sought.

The far bank sloped more shallowly, and beyond it he could see the grasses of the open prairie bent by the steady light wind. The sky was an immense bowl above him, a just-perceptible darker tone to the east marking the progress of the afternoon. The water rippled musically over the pebbles in the shallows and moved with sinuous power in the deeper center of the stream. Upstream there was an arrangement of planks laid on the shore, a vestigial dock with two light rowboats moored to it, sterns pointing downstream like the Nonpareil's wind vanes. In the other direction there was nothing visible of human works, and Brandon supposed that an Indian fifty years ago, or a thousand years ago, would have seen the same scene from this point. I could walk along here and be out of my time, out of my self, he thought. A little way along and I wouldn't have to be Brandon or Blake or any of them, just a man by the river.

He rounded a bend, pushed his way through some stiff young green reeds, and stopped as he saw that he was no longer alone. A man sat leaning against the grassy bank ahead of him, holding a bamboo fishing rod with its line trailing in the water.

At the noise of Brandon's passage through the reeds the fisherman looked up with a start that set the rod quivering.

"Mr. Kingslake," Brandon said.

"Oh . . . oh, it's you, Mr. Blake. The, uh, you travel in . . ."

"Windmills," Brandon said.

"Of course, windmills, I couldn't for the moment think . . . You followed me here?"

"No," Brandon said. "Just walking, found my way."

"No, you wouldn't, of course, not you. Why would you follow me?"

The newspaperman looked even older and more haunted than he had peering out of his office the day he had published his groveling recantation. Whatever the vigilantes had done to him, Brandon thought, they haven't stopped doing it.

"You can't keep giving in all along the line," Brandon said gently. "They'll always go on pushing you until there's nowhere left to go, and then, when you have to resist, it'll be the wrong place and the wrong time. You can't do it on your own, but there's many a man in town will stand with you if you'll let them."

Kingslake's pale eyes searched Brandon's face as if to see if there were any chance of making a claim that he had no idea what Brandon was talking about. Then he sighed and said, "You don't know."

"What did they do?" Brandon asked.

"They hurt me. Pushed my arm to just short of dislocation. It hurt worse than anything I ever felt, and I knew that one more touch and it would hurt ten times worse, and I'd likely be a cripple. One of them knew what I'm like about pain—I'm a coward, d'you see? It's that simple, a coward about pain, and it don't matter most of the time, my line of work, so most don't get to know about it, but he does—and he had them do that and tell me what worse they'd do. And I set and printed that handbill and got it out."

"And so they let you alone," Brandon said.

Kingslake shook his head. "They like to have fun. They tell me what they're up to, who they beat, what they'll do next. And they know I can't print it or tell anyone, for I know what they'd do to me if I did. It's like filling a sack with more sand than it'll hold. It'll stretch, the stitches will start to pull, and finally it'll burst. They tell me things, and not being able to tell is pulling me apart. But telling would mean worse than being pulled apart that way. If I tell what they tell me, they'll hurt me, and I could not make my tongue and mouth work to do that any more than I could fly."

"You know who they are, then," Brandon said.

"I didn't say that," Kingslake said anxiously.

"But you do. Damn it, man, if you told me, told Chief Hodge, we could break that crowd up in an hour, and you'd be safe."

"If I told you who they are, could you and Hodge and Lunney go and kill them where you find them?"

Brandon blinked. "Well, no. Arrest them, probably take them to Platteville for trial, the lawful way."

"Then they'd be able to hurt me, and they'd find a way to do it," Kingslake said. "I can't tell you."

"You could help the town, maybe save it from something bad, save people's lives, Kingslake—isn't that enough to make you tell me who the vigilantes are?"

"No," Kingslake said. "If you hurt me, I probably would tell you."

The sudden twist of nausea Brandon felt came at least partly from the brief impulse he had to follow Kingslake's lead. It is always interesting, he thought next, to come up against a situation that shows you just where one of your limits is. I guess torture isn't a bad place to stop short of.

"Do you know where they get together, if they have a regular meeting place?" he said. "At least maybe you could tell me that."

Kingslake shook his head. "I can't tell you anything. I am a coward, Blake. You have to understand what that means. I can imagine in every detail what pain I haven't experienced is like, and I can remember every pain that's been inflicted on me. There isn't anything that can induce me to risk going through what they did to me again, let alone anything new. The words would just not come out of my mouth."

Brandon looked at the arching sky and the tall grass, and then at the twisted figure of the sitting man, a man with all the immensity of creation around him, but imprisoned in his tiny self by his fears.

"I can't tell you where they meet, Blake, so put that out of your mind, put the whole business out of your mind," Kingslake said with a shrill note in his voice. "We'll talk of your windmills, maybe. How they'll help the farmers, bring water to the crops. That'll be good, won't it, higher yield per acre?"

Kingslake was babbling, but Brandon had the sense that it was very important to listen to what he would say.

"Windmills can make a difference if there's a drought, that's true. But can they do anything against the grass-hoppers, Blake? If the hoppers come again, why, then the crops are done, and the farmers are damned. Unless there's a miracle. There was a miracle once, a miracle that saved the farmers from the hoppers." Kingslake stared at Brandon with eyes so wide that the whites showed all around the irises. "Go away and let me fish in peace, I've told you nothing, and I'll tell you nothing."

Brandon turned and walked back upstream toward where he had climbed down the bank. For a coward, Kingslake had just done something brave, outwitting his terrified body to hint at what he dared not say. And it made sense. Remote from scrutiny and approachable by stealth, an ideal meeting place for the secret group poisoning Bigsbee with fear: the deserted Seagull saloon, named for the hungry birds that had once saved the farmers from the grasshoppers.

Brandon had first thought to reconnoiter the Seagull in daylight, but he realized that the north edge had regained some of its population, which would be firmly in the vigilante camp. When it was dark enough so that he would at best be seen as an unrecognizable figure in the unlit streets, he made his way to the north edge and, keeping well clear of the few buildings showing lights, to the Seagull. He had no clear expectation of what his investigation would show him but thought that going over the saloon might give him some indication of whether he had interpreted Kingslake's disjointed discourse correctly. After that, perhaps he and Rattner, and perhaps Ed Marks, could work out what to do with the information.

As Brandon approached the Seagull, however, he saw a faint gleam of light in a window toward the rear of the first floor. He kept well away from the building until he was abreast of the window, then moved slowly toward it, careful to set each foot to the ground toe downward, probing for a rock or piece of wood whose displacement would make a carrying noise. He wondered if leaving his .38 behind had been all that sensible an idea but decided that his best weapons were still stealth and painstaking care.

As he approached the window it appeared to rise above him, and he saw that a ditch ran beside the building so that he could not see over the sill. He closed his eyes and remembered the Seagull as he had seen it the day of Jere Sublette's hanging. Yes, the crowd had come from that direction, and he had seen the side of the building before they reached the front. Three windows, the rearmost of which he was now standing under, and, yes, at the rear corner a rickety-looking barrel that once, when all its staves were in place, had held rain.

He stepped to the rear slowly, hands stretched before him, and touched the rough, gently curving surface of the barrel's staves and the cooler metal of its hoops. He found a space where a slat had once been, inserted his hands, and tugged it toward him. It made a faint scraping sound as he dragged it over the earth, and he nearly tripped and fell as he lifted it and tried to carry it. Near the window he eased it over onto its side and then pulled it upright so that it stood bottom upward.

Grabbing the projecting windowsill, he hooked one leg over the top of the barrel and levered himself upward with a clattering and scraping that seemed loud to him but apparently did not carry very far. At least, when he was able to crouch on the barrel top and peer through the window, he did not seem to have disturbed the deliberations of the men grouped around a table inside the saloon.

There were six of them, indistinctly lit by a lantern set on the table, and the grouping seemed like a burlesque of the town council. The short man who appeared to be in charge said something in a choleric voice that identified him as Geary, even though the light was so faint that his face was not clear. Well, no, Brandon thought, they wouldn't wear masks to their own meetings, would they?

The window was closed, and the voices of the men inside and seated at the other side of the room came to him not much more strongly than the buzzing of flies. He eased forward to see if placing his ear against the pane would let him hear more distinctly, then stopped the motion as one of the men reached forward and turned the lantern up. As the light strengthened he saw Geary's face clearly, and also a beaky profile and a wide-mouthed head, and other less distinctive but still recognizable faces.

It was no wonder the vigilante committee had reminded Brandon of the town council. Except for being under the direction of Geary rather than Danby, it *was* the town council.

Brandon did not know whether he had made a sudden move in response to this revelation or whether the decrepit barrel had coincidentally reached the end of its powers of cohesion, but the bottom on which he was crouched gave way on one side, dropping his leg into the interior of the barrel and trapping him painfully.

He stifled a shout of surprise and pain, but the unbalanced barrel toppled, throwing him with a thump against the side of the building and then carrying him to the bottom of the ditch and a dazing meeting of his head with a rock.

He was trying to thrash his way loose from the grasping staves of the barrel when he heard the sound of shouts and running feet, louder and closer, and then the kicks that struck stabs of pain through his side and chest and slammed into his head with a burst of fire that turned into soft and welcome darkness.

19

Brandon's first emotion on regaining consciousness was an unfocused regret. It assumed clarity as he realized that what he was regretting was how he was going to feel when he became fully aware again. He could tell that it was going to be pretty bad.

It was. His head throbbed, feeling as if a logger's wedge had been pounded into it and was being struck regularly; his ribs and belly ached, the pain sharpening as he breathed; breathing itself was laborious and painful, the air rasping through a swollen nose. The inside of his mouth felt raw, probably gashed by his own teeth as the flesh was smashed against them by a fist or boot. Sucking air over the torn flesh would have hurt, but the cloth wadded in his mouth and secured by some binding around his head kept that, at least, from being a problem.

He started to raise his hands to push the gag away and felt the cold grip of metal at his wrists. He bent his elbows to bring his hands into view and saw that they were secured with rusty handcuffs.

Brandon became aware that he was lying on his side on a dirt floor. He knew what he needed to know about his immediate state—all bad—and now started to examine his surroundings.

He was toward one side of a room about fifteen feet square, rather larger than Carl Swanson's back room but even more simply furnished, with only a crude wooden bed frame crisscrossed with sagging ropes and an open bucket in one corner. The walls appeared to be constructed of railroad ties studded with the heads of bolts. In one side was a door with no handle or knob visible; in the other was a small window with close-set steel bars between half an inch and an inch thick.

The jail at the far western edge of town—that's what it had to be, he concluded.

Brandon bent his legs and thrashed back and forward and sideways until he heaved himself up on his knees, then struggled to his feet. He lost balance and almost toppled over, but the wall stopped his fall at the cost of some moderate agony, and he was able to slide his way upright.

The window was set high, but he could see out of it. It faced the open prairie to the west, with not a building in sight. The sky was hazed with a yellowish gray, and it was impossible to tell by sun location or shadows what the time of day was. About ten yards from the building was a scrubby tree with a crude wooden bench under it. On it sat a man holding a shotgun. Brandon thought he looked like one of the vigilantes' guards from the station platform; even if he wasn't, it was clear that he was the same kind of man, and doing the same job. If I slip out of the cuffs, get the gag off, and, say, unscrew the bolts with my teeth so as to make a hole in the wall, he thought, why, then he can drop me in my tracks. No wonder they need him.

After a moment he realized that the guard was not to prevent him from escaping, but to deflect any thought any Bigsbeans might entertain about an idle stroll to the jail. The guard wouldn't be visible enough from town to attract curiosity but would have ample notice of any intruders.

Deathwind

Brandon moved back from the window and leaned against the wall. Considering his situation was dismaying, but if he concentrated on it hard enough, he would forget how much he hurt, which was some gain.

First, he had succeeded completely in his mission of finding out who the Vigilante Committee was: Geary and the town council.

Second, the success was at the moment worthless. He had no way of making the information known to Rattner or anyone else.

Third, the prospect of amending the second circumstance for the better was dim, if you considered midnight a dim time of night. The jail hadn't held Jere Sublette long, but Sublette had had friends who knew where he was and had the sand to free him, unfortunately without seriously damaging the jail in the process. Calvin Blake had a few helpful-minded friends who had no idea in the world where he was or any notion that he was in danger. Simon Rattner would assume he was back at the Kitson farm, and the Kitsons would assume that some matter of business had kept him in town. He doubted that Helen Kitson would be paying much attention to whether he was there or not anyhow. Ed Marks might wonder why Brandon had not retrieved the saddle horse, but it was impossible to guess how long it would take him to think there might be a sinister explanation for that. Brandon estimated that he did not have much time.

They didn't kill me on the spot last night because they wanted time to work out how the body ought to look when it was found, he decided. Broken neck, thrown from a horse? Something like that. They're still a little shy of open murder; that might get the townsfolk scared enough to go beyond being scared and fight back, and they're not strong enough to deal with that yet.

But they'll work out what they mean to do, and when it's dark again they'll come for me and do it. I've seen them, and they can't let me live. They're caught up in this, and they can't let it go.

It makes sense, he thought. Five council members,

fellows who got the job because nobody else wanted it, not enough backbone among them to do anything except what Danby tells them to. Everybody calls them Mr. Councilman to their faces and mocks them behind their backs. And then this thing with Sublette blows up, and crazy Geary comes to them, says they can really run things here instead of just seeming to; nobody'll be laughing then. Give weak men power, and you have the worst kind of tyranny. They'll have to kill me . . . and if they do, I'll never know if one of them's Farmer Dick.

From the beginning of his quest Cole Brandon had known that it could well end prematurely with his own death, and he had experienced both the near-certainty of being killed before his next heartbeat and the drawn-out waiting for equally probable but excruciatingly deferred dying. He had never been anything like at ease under such circumstances, but he had borne them with enough fortitude to take whatever action was necessary or possible.

Now he was filled with a sick wave of dread, a sensation that seemed almost physical rather than emotional. The hair seemed to lift on the back of his neck, and he paced uneasily around the cell, turning his head and sniffing the air.

You are acting like a caged animal, Counselor, he thought, and you can't control it. You've been in bad spots before; what is it about this one that's got you so scared?

He stopped as he realized that *he*—that the mind of Cole Brandon and the troupe of alter egos traveling in his body—was not afraid. It was the body, the vehicle, that was reacting, yes, like an animal.

Brandon sniffed again and caught a sharp tang in the air. He walked to the window, made ungainly by the enforced stillness of the arms cuffed in front of him.

The nearby sky was pearl-gray, but a little to the west was a moving mountain of deep gray and inky black, swelling as it rushed eastward. There was no farmhouse visible, but otherwise the scene bore a distinct resem-

blance to the photograph of the oncoming tornado Carl
Swanson had been foolish enough to take.

The resemblance became even closer as a nebulous
shape appeared at the lower portion of the onrushing
cloud bank, thickened, then formed itself into a kind of
elephant's trunk, probing at the ground below.

It did not appear to move, just to grow larger, which
Brandon realized meant that it was heading in a dead
straight line for the jail. The atmosphere, charged with
electricity by the violence of the storm, was clearly the
cause of the unreasoning sensation of physical fear he
had experienced. Now I know that, Brandon thought, I
have something I can really panic about.

The guard had risen from the bench and, as Brandon
watched, turned and ran toward the jail and passed out
of sight.

Son of a bitch could have stopped and opened the
door, Brandon thought bitterly, given me a chance to get
away from that twister. But if he was the kind that'd do
that, would he have that job?

The tornado funnel was twice as large as when he first
saw it, and visibly swelling as he watched. He could see
spiral bands of lighter gray in the wider upper portion,
and a churning cloud of dust where the tip dragged
across the ground.

Brandon threw himself to the floor and scratched at
the earth with his fingernails. Damn it, Counselor, you
can't dig a cyclone cellar in the time you've got! Sure, but
better die scratching than die doing nothing.

A glare of unearthly yellow light struck through the
window. Brandon heard a sound like four express trains
converging on him; the air seemed to turn to a jellylike
solid around him, then to a vacuum that pulled the
breath from his lungs, and the jail exploded as if a mine
had been detonated under it.

Brandon was deafened and dazed but felt strangely
still. He opened his eyes and saw shimmering blacks and
grays—then a rapidly revolving patch of ground some
distance off.

Nearby some lengths of timber with splintered ends moved slowly, as if drifting with him in some river eddy. A stiff-legged horse standing on nothing but ropes of whirling cloud glared at him from perhaps twenty feet away. Above him in a black, howling void spidery trees of pure light branched back and forth across the walls of the funnel.

Dead and in hell, Brandon thought; then he realized that he, like the horse and the fragments of the jail, had been caught up in the tornado. He remembered the second picture in Carl Swanson's set, showing a timber driven through a tree, and decided that his first estimate was only premature, not inaccurate. It would not matter if the tornado drove him through a tree or just partway into it; the overall result would be the same.

Though he could hardly breathe, he felt strangely calm, cocooned in superthickened air while the earth spun below him and the lightning raved above. Then fear clutched at him as the invisible bonds about him seemed to loosen, the ground rose toward him, and he felt himself spinning through the air till he was struck a stunning blow by what felt like a giant's hammer.

In a moment he realized that what had hit him was even larger: the entire planet, in fact. He breathed shallowly, face pressed to the ground, for some moments, then lifted his head and watched the tornado retreating. It had shifted its track northward, skipping the main part of Bigsbee; the north edge of town seemed to have a kind of trough cut through it, though the landmark bulk of the Seagull still loomed above its surroundings.

He rolled over and lay on his back, looking up at the ragged streaks of cloud, admiring them as if they were the most delicate of sunsets. Right now anything looked beautiful. He got to his hands and knees, realizing that the freakish power of the twister had slid the cuffs from his wrists, leaving not even a scrape behind. He reached up, tore the gag from his mouth, and gratefully drew in a deep breath.

Being alive was enough of a surprise that the disappearance of the handcuffs did not seem a great further improbability. Even seeing the horse, his recent neighbor in the tornado, placidly grazing nearby was not particularly astonishing.

A hundred yards or so beyond it a fan of heavy timber and a leafless tree marked the start of Brandon's journey. Brandon glanced toward Bigsbee and saw no one coming out to investigate the ruins of the jail. If he got out of here quickly, he figured, the vigilantes would surely assume that he had been reduced to fragments by the twister, or possibly taken up to heaven like Elijah, either way no further danger to them.

A chill wind out of the west slammed raindrops into him so hard that he thought for a moment they were hail. There was a heavy curtain all around him now, and the rain roared as it drummed on the ground.

Brandon walked over to the horse and, wincing at what the effort did to his bruised body, clambered onto its back. Thirty miles or so without a saddle was not an attractive prospect, but it beat his most recent mode of travel. The rain would make finding his way hard, but it would cut down on the chances of the vigilantes' sentries seeing him. He headed the horse south, considering that the far side of the river, even if it were the longer way to Platteville, would be safer.

The rain thinned a little, and he could see a scatter of trees marking the edge of the river ahead. A crack like a coastal cannon being fired deafened him at the same instant that the tallest of the trees became a cloud of steam and splinters at the bottom of a blue-white rope of light that flashed from the black sky.

Brandon contemplated the idea of being for some hours the tallest object on the open prairie in this kind of storm, then set the horse scrambling down the riverbank.

Keep down here, he thought, and lightning won't likely be attracted, but it'd be a good idea to lie flat on the horse's neck. We can keep to the river a good bit of the way to Platteville. .... He remembered the sight of the cool creek from the train and amended the thought: damn near all the way.

The horse picked its way gingerly through the shallows, unsteady on the shifting footing the pebbles afforded, and Brandon wondered if he could hold on if it suddenly stumbled. The shape he was in, being thrown from horseback onto rocks would not be a good idea.

The horse plodded around a bend, and Brandon saw the planking dock and the two boats he had seen the day before, and looked past them to the swift current of the rain-fed river.

He climbed down from the horse, patted the side of its head, and said, "Horse, find your way back to wherever the twister kidnapped you from, and good luck to you."

Brandon inspected the boats, chose the one with the widest seat board, and overturned it to empty out the rainwater, setting the oars to one side. He slipped the bow rope from around the tree stump that secured it, set the oars back in the boat, stepped in, eased himself down to the seat, then leaned a leg over the side and dug his boot into the shore to push off.

The boat shuddered out into the current, and Brandon used one oar like a rudder to point the bow downstream. Then he lay back, knees up, and let the gentle rocking motion of the boat and the silent, rapid passage past him of the river's banks soothe him. He was wet through, bruised, and steadily pelted by the downpour, but he felt supremely alive and exhilarated as the river drew him into the roaring curtain of rain.

20

"A warrant, duly signed and attested, for the arrest of Saul Geary, merchant of this town, on charges of battery and unlawful imprisonment," Sheriff Cameron said. "That's all I've got a sworn witness for, Mr. Blake here, but it'll hold him till we get enough to try him for sedition, aggravated assault, and so on. And here's five more with the names to be filled in, since I never troubled to learn the names of your damn city council."

Chief Hodge was still in the daze that had come upon him with Cameron's irruption into his office, followed by six men in sober suits carrying heavy rifles and ammunition boxes and a battered-looking windmill salesman. "The council?" he said.

"Blake saw 'em confabulating with Geary in a place where the vigilantes are known to meet, and they knocked him out and threw him into your jail till they could decide how to kill him," Cameron said impatiently. "I told you that once, and you don't need any clearer proof than that. Write in the damn names, and we'll go get 'em and take 'em off your hands."

Brandon was still a little adrift himself; Cameron, roused to action, had that effect on most people. Arriving the day before in Platteville, soaked through and muddy from a half-mile walk through sodden fields, he had expected a lot of uphill work in persuading Cameron to believe his story, or even, given his present state, to let him begrime the sheriff's office.

Instead, Cameron had listened intently, then slammed his hand on his desk, imperiling the balance of the metal inkwell. "Insurrection!" he said. "I smelled it there, like brimstone! Those two-faced serpents, subverting the lawful authority of the town like butter wouldn't melt in their mouths."

Brandon pushed away the picture of fanged jaws closing around lumps of butter. "Look at it one way, they *are* the lawful authority there."

"Not when they subvert themselves," Cameron said. "Insurrection's insurrection and sedition's sedition, no matter who by or against. A dog bites me or his own tail, he's still a biter. That wiseacre Danby, the council chairman, he one of them?"

"No," Brandon said. "Looks as if Geary saw the rest of them resented Danby and stepped in to take advantage of that. Danby's full of himself, but he's honest and, far as I know, behaves lawful and orderly at all times." Maybe, Brandon mused, because he hasn't had John B. Parker's throat under his razor yet, of course. . . .

Cameron briskly saw to his preparations, including getting Brandon housed for the night and cleaned up, and by noon the next day he had the warrants for Geary and five John Does drawn up and approved by a judge, had assembled half a dozen hard-faced and heavily armed deputies, and was waiting with them and Brandon at the Platteville station.

Given the confusion caused by the cyclone and the fact that the vigilantes seemed to have paid less attention to westbound trains than to eastbound ones that could carry talkative passengers to the county seat, Brandon guessed that there would be no guards waiting for them, and there were not. As the eight men walked toward

Chief Hodge's office a few men stared, and two walked quickly away, vanishing into narrow northward streets.

Now Hodge, looking a little wild-eyed, seemed to accept that the impossible had happened—a tornado running through the town you live in can expand your ideas of what can and cannot happen—or at least that a higher authority claimed it had, so that he could not be blamed if anything went wrong. He filled in the councilmen's names on the John Doe warrants, handed them back to Cameron, and stood up. "Geary first, I expect. I'll take you to his store. You come along, Lunney."

The constable pulled himself back from his awed contemplation of the deputies, whose businesslike wool suits made them look a good deal more menacing than the most extravagantly ragged and bloody desperado, and buckled on his pistol belt.

The sight of the ten men moving purposefully down Main Street created brief eddies of onlookers who clumped together to look and discuss, then seemed to realize that the posse was looking for the kind of trouble that resulted in the air being crisscrossed with flying lead slugs and melted away.

Geary's clerk said with the earnestness of deep alarm that Mr. Geary had been away for two hours at least, not saying where he was going or when he would be back.

The undertaker, Connor, was also absent and unaccounted for. To Brandon's surprise, it seemed that Connor was the toadlike man. The somber vulturine one was Morton, the dentist; like Geary and Connor—and, Cameron and Hodge soon found out, the other three councilmen—he was not at his place of business or any other place anyone appeared to know about.

"Well, you saw them at this Seagull place," Cameron said to Brandon. "Might's well look for them there as anywhere."

Hodge and Brandon exchanged glances, remembering the last time a body of men had marched on the Seagull.

Cameron and Hodge walked at the head of the group, with Brandon not quite between and not quite behind them. The six deputies carried their rifles loosely but ready to be brought into play instantly. Brandon thought they were .45 or .50 caliber, like the ones the buffalo hunters preferred for their ability to drop one of the massive beasts as a .22 does a squirrel, and that anyone who argued with a battery of six of them was even more lunatic than the vigilantes had so far shown themselves to be. Brandon was carrying a .38 borrowed from Chief Hodge. His brief regret that he had not brought his own pistol into town with him the day before yesterday vanished when he considered the likelihood of the Vigilance Committee or the tornado having left it on him.

Lunney trotted at the end with his pistol out, looking from side to side and making a point of not responding to the startled glances of the Bigsbeans they passed.

Ed Marks, sitting outside his stable, saw Brandon, got up, and fell into step beside him. "When you didn't come back for your horse the other day, thought the twister might have got you. What's the parade?"

"It did. Sheriff's men out to arrest the vigilantes." Brandon explained the situation to Ed Marks, who whistled. "Some doings for a windmill salesman, Blake. Yeah, it makes sense they'd be holed up at the Seagull now; they'd have had word the sheriff's coming for 'em, and they'd want to get together and work out what to do about it. Damn, that is one for the books. Geary, he's no surprise, for he's always been a little cracked on law and order, but the others I wouldn't have expected it of. I guess the masks made it seem safe, though there's some that like to have it known who's doing the job—the James boys out east and the like."

Gren Kenneally didn't wear a mask either, Brandon thought; that predatory eagle's beak and glaring eye would terrify a victim into immobility better than any mask.

"You, there!" Cameron said over his shoulder. "Are you armed?"

Ed Marks patted the side of his trousers. "Got a shooter about, yes, Sheriff."

"He trustworthy, Blake?"

"Absolutely," Brandon said.

"You're deputized, then. Come on—you'll recognize these damn insurrectionists sooner'n I will."

Cameron turned and strode on. Marks turned to Brandon and said, "Can he do that?"

Brandon jerked a thumb over his shoulder. "He's backed by six men with buffalo guns, not counting Lunney, if they don't make the point."

"I guess he can," Marks said. "Well, it sets easier with me to be going after these fellows than after poor old Jere."

The early dusk did not much soften the spectacle of the destruction the cyclone had brought to the north edge of Bigsbee. It looked as though a giant garden roller had been run across much of the district, flattening houses as though they had been made of cards, after which an equally monstrous hay rake had been dragged across the path of devastation, tearing and tangling the fragmented buildings and creating windrows of broken timber.

The twister had neatly avoided the Seagull, which stood smugly intact like one of those churches or orphan asylums spared by a beneficent providence that the papers loved to run engravings of after a natural disaster.

Just as there had been before, there was a group of people standing in front of the saloon. This time, as the sheriff's men approached, they scattered quickly, leaving the space in front of the building vacant. Brandon saw that the window Jere Sublette had gone through had two planks nailed across it.

Brandon was picking out a pile of timber to use as a firing position when Cameron lifted up his hand and brought his group to a stop.

Hodge voiced Brandon's thought, saying, "Shouldn't we be taking cover in case they're in there?"

"That's not how you deal with insurrection," Cameron said. He cupped his hands around his mouth and bawled. "In the name of the State of Nebraska and the County of McGaha! I call on Saul Geary and all purported members of the so-called Committee of Vigilance to surrender themselves to the duly constituted authorities of said state and county, here marshaled!"

"How's he know they're in there?" Ed Marks muttered.

Smoke, a wink of flame, and the crack of a pistol shot came from one of the upstairs windows. "That's how," Brandon said. The bullet seemed to have gone nowhere near him, and he could hear shouts, either of defiance at the sheriff or remonstrance at the incautious gunman.

Cameron did not, as Brandon strongly felt like doing, dive for the natural forts provided by the debris but raised his hand and chopped it down. The six deputies brought their rifles up and fired a staggered volley that hit Brandon's ears harder than the thunderclap accompanying the lightning that had almost fried him yesterday.

The upper story of the Seagull had sprouted a rash of large black dots, and one section of siding was hanging loose. The shouts redoubled in force, but there were no screams or moans among them. Brandon supposed that Cameron's men were trained to send their first shots high, to allow a few instants' reflection on surrender.

Cameron raised his arm straight, made a pumping motion, and ran toward the Seagull's front door. Knowing that the men behind him were already in motion, and that he had the choices of sprinting after Cameron, leaping nimbly to one side, or being trampled underfoot, Brandon took the first course; so did Ed Marks.

Inside the saloon Cameron pounded toward and up the stairs. "Goes up 'most as fast as we come down," Ed Marks gasped.

Brandon heard the drumming of the deputies' shoes on the floorboards, loud and menacing as the hoofbeats of stampeding cattle, and scrambled up the stairs.

As he reached the top a man sprang at him, holding a pistol that seemed centered on his left eye, and fired.

Brandon was blinded by the muzzle flash and fell back; he heard another explosion from behind him, and then Ed Marks grabbed him and pulled him to one side as the deputies pounded past to follow Cameron to the front of the building.

When Brandon's vision cleared he was aware of Constable Lunney on one side of him and Ed Marks on the other. Marks was breathing hard and holding his gun loosely; smoke wisped up from it.

"I had to . . . he was gonna shoot again, Blake. You saw it, didn't you, Lunney?"

"Yah," the constable said. "No choice, Ed. But, Jesus . . ."

Brandon looked down at the man who writhed on the floor, holding both hands pressed to his belly without stanching the flow of dark blood that pulsed between his fingers. His staring eyes seemed to look past Brandon, and his face was distorted with pain, with fear, and still perhaps with a killing rage, but it was easily recognizable as Walter Kitson's face.

"Blake!" he said hoarsely. "Come close—got to talk to you!"

There were shouts, but no shots, from the front room; Brandon supposed that he would not be needed in whatever remained to be done with the just-deposed vigilantes.

"Walter," he said, "how'd this happen? What an awful mistake! We'll get the doc and—"

"Doc!" A bubble of blood accompanied the word out of Walter Kitson's mouth and burst, filming his chin and lips with red. "Past time for docs. No mistake, Blake . . . lean close, don't want others t' hear . . . too shaming. Found those pictures, your buggy . . ."

Brandon gestured to Lunney and Ed Marks to move away and thought, Oh, shit, I put them in there for safekeeping and kept them so safe I forgot about them. Must have exploded that poor bastard's mind like a charge of dynamite.

They had. The pictures of his aunt, not only naked but

clearly lustfully inclined toward the camera operator, had sent Walter Kitson into a state beyond rage, sent him into frenzied action, impelled by random gusts of impulse and passion.

"Got ax, was gonna kill 'em both when I found 'em, then I dropped it, couldn' hurt her, no matter what she . . . Then I come to the north edge, said I needed the Committee, knew something they needed to know, so someone brought me here, and I was telling 'em where they could find Swanson, and then there was all that shouting and shooting outside, and you come busting in, and when I saw you I wanted to kill you . . ."

Walter Kitson's words were being filtered through a steady bubbling sound now, and Brandon had to lean closer to hear them. "Why?"

Kitson glared at him. "You saw the pictures, saw her naked. . . . *I . . . never . . . did!*"

His eyes opened wider, and his jaw went slack, and he gave a single great shudder as if trying to throw off painful bonds, and then he went limp and seemed to shrink into stillness on the red-stained floor.

Brandon stood up and walked to where Ed Marks and Lunney were standing. The five town councilmen and Geary stumbled toward them in handcuffs, prodded along by the somberly suited deputies and followed by Sheriff Cameron.

Cameron paused by Walter Kitson's body and looked at Brandon. "Farmer, name of Kitson," Brandon said. "Doing some sleuthing on his own, got a line on the committee, made the mistake of coming here to spy on them. When we came in he lost his head and shot at us, nearly killed me and was going to shoot again; Marks had to drop him. Damn shame, but no way out of it."

This was near enough what had happened so that neither Lunney nor Ed Marks felt like contradicting it, but it left enough unexplained so that both had a tinge of dubiousness in their expressions.

Sheriff Cameron squinted at them shrewdly, then seemed to decide that whatever irregularity there might be, it had nothing to do with sedition and insurrection and so was not worth pursuing.

Helen Kitson and Carl Swanson, having only Brandon's account to go on, were even more easily persuaded of its truth. Helen was shaken with grief and mourning, but not stricken by them, and Carl Swanson was shocked; but it was clear that both realized that once mourning and shock were done with, so was the one obstacle to their union, or at least to the open expression of it.

Carl Swanson also found that he had, at least for the moment, left the painting and photography business and was pitchforked into farming. "We don't want to do this forever," Helen Kitson said the morning after Brandon had returned to the farm with his news, "and we'll sell it off when we can. But we've got to sell a working farm, not a piece of abandoned land, and that means we have to work it. I can do a lot of things women don't usually do, and I will, but you'll have to do an awful lot of things you're not used to, Carl . . . and you will."

Carl Swanson looked at Helen Kitson with devotion and adoration and that faint unease apparent on the faces of most men who have just achieved their heart's desire.

"I've been thinking for a while about moving into Bigsbee," said Brandon, to whom the idea had just suggested itself. "I've sold all the windmills I'm going to, and all I have to do now is wait for the ones on order to come in and help install them; I don't have to be out here to go calling on other farmers. And in town I'd be handy to the bank so I can talk to Mr. Rattner about loans if I have to."

About half of this collection of reasons was valid, and Brandon considered the ones he had not given even more so. He had not killed Walter Kitson (and Helen Kitson could not know the contribution his carelessness had made to his death), but he had been involved, and his presence would be a jarring reminder. Also, Helen

Kitson and Carl Swanson were so much a couple that a third party on hand could not but seem intrusive, particularly a third party as aware of Helen Kitson's sensual appeal as Brandon was.

Helen Kitson said farewell to Brandon with a combination of affection and regret and an unstated acknowledgment of his tact in leaving her and Carl Swanson to their own devices.

Carl Swanson shook Brandon's hand as he leaned down from the buggy and said, "It's wonderful how it's all turned out, in spite of poor Walter. Helen, the farm, everything a man could want. But . . . I guess I'm not going to see the photography building at the Centennial Exposition, am I?"

It was a measure of the return to normality of Bigsbee that, once the former town council and Geary had been removed to Platteville and a temporary three-man body chosen by Danby, Rattner, and Chief Hodge chosen to stand in for them, with elections for a full replacement body scheduled to be held in a month's time, the talk of the town reverted to its favorite topics, the Centennial and the iniquities and inequities of the railroad companies, particularly the one serving Bigsbee.

"I could go," Ed Marks told Brandon, "and it would be a wonder, the Exposition, the horses and machines that I'm interested in, everything. You know, I come here to try farming, but I saw that what with freight rates sky-high and the best land taken, I wouldn't do any good at it, so I went into the livery. Like I said, hiring out to work with my own teams of horses and machines, that'd put together the things I know best, horses and farming, so the Exposition would show me lots I could profit by knowing, and sometimes I think I will go to it, then I think I won't, then will again. But it's a long trip by stage and boat, and I don't like trains—they're bad luck, and so much can go wrong with 'em. And I learned there's money owed me in Philadelphia, so I should go get it, but some kinds of money, it's not worth it, so it's I won't go again. . . . You ever get to wondering if you should be doing what you're doing, Blake?"

No, you don't, do you, Counselor? he asked. Because you have an idea of what could happen if you did wonder about it, don't you?

"I guess not," Ed Marks said. "Windmills, there's not much to wonder about. You sell 'em or you don't, and if you don't, you're not doing it much longer. If I don't make a change with this business, I won't be doing it much longer, neither. I don't want to go to Philadelphia for the money I'm owed, but I need money if I'm to move up into machines and the horses to pull them, so I'll have to look for other ways to find that. There should be a pavilion at the Exposition for fellows that need to lay hands on a chunk of money but don't know whereat it is."

Simon Rattner, it turned out, cherished an ambition to visit the Art Annex and the statues and paintings in the different national pavilions. "I lived in New York once, and you could see pictures and sculpture all the time, but out here it's nothing but engravings in the papers, and maybe a crayon drawing by somebody like Swanson. I want to sink myself in that stuff for a while, soak it up so's I can remember it in the dry years out here."

Swicegood was active in getting up a party of Grangers who were seeing if they could scrape up the train fare and find a couple of weeks of free time to take in the spectacle. "The National Grange has worked a fine deal," he said. "Leased a spot outside Philadelphia and put up a sort of city where you can stay for half a dollar a night and the same for any meals, and real cheap rates on the railroad to and from the fair. It'd be a shame and a sin to miss it."

Like Ed Marks, but for a different cause, he regretted that the best way to Philadelphia was the train: "It gripes me to pay our good money for fares to John B. Parker and the like, when it's them that are doing their best to see we don't have that money. I don't know how long we're going to stand for it. Also don't know what we can do if we decide *not* to stand for it, more's the pity. There's a meeting tomorrow of farmers from hereabouts, Grangers and those that haven't joined, to see if there's anything, a strike or something like that. You might want to look in, say hello to the fellows you sold those windmills to."

"An idea," Brandon said, not adding that it seemed like not a particularly good one.

In fact he compromised by being part of the group of bystanders by the open door of the Grange Hall, nodding to men he knew as they went in and listening to the aggrieved and predictable opening remarks.

When the meeting was well launched, without any indication of anything startling or useful to come, Brandon drifted away. The first westbound train of the day was due shortly, and the last two Nonpareils he had transmitted orders for were due about now. Once they were installed, he would have to decide if it was worthwhile staying in Bigsbee to hunt for Farmer Dick. All of the arrested vigilantes had been in Bigsbee for at least three years without enough of an absence to have participated in the Mound Farm killings with Gren Kenneally, and no other prospects had appeared. On the other hand, he had that gut certainty that the man he sought was somewhere around. With that sort of reasoning at work he certainly couldn't afford to wonder if he should be doing what he was doing, as Ed Marks had wondered if he did.

Brandon positioned himself at the front of the platform, where the baggage car would stop. When its doors opened he did not need the clerk's confirmation to know that there were no wooden-crated Nonpareils aboard; if there, they were highly prominent.

He turned away from the baggage car and saw two passengers descending from the last car. The first, a slender man wearing a derby hat, looked somewhat familiar; he turned and took a valise from the more substantial man coming down the stairs behind him, who was much more familiar, because more recently seen, and who also prompted the identification of the first man.

This was Jake Trexler, the railroad detective who had accompanied Cole Brandon to the scene of his wife's murder at Mound Farm and later served as bodyguard to John B. Parker, who now stood on the platform beside him.

A man standing beside Brandon stiffened and said, "Hey, I seen that fellow, the fat one with the nose. I seen his picture in the papers. Palmer, ain't it?"

"John B. Parker," Brandon said.

The man looked at him and said, "Thass a lie. John B. Parker wouldn't come here, a big railroad man like that."

"It's his railroad, and it stops here. I guess he can take a notion to do the same," Brandon said. "I've met him, and that's John B. Parker, all right."

Brandon instantly realized that it might have been a good idea to let the new arrival's alias of Palmer stand when the man said, "Hot *damn*" and ran across the street and into the Grange Hall.

21

John B. Parker and Jake Trexler looked up as Brandon approached them on the platform.

"Mr. Parker, Mr. Trexler," he said. "A while since I've had the pleasure of meeting you—Calvin Blake, if you recall. What brings you to Bigsbee?"

"Hello, there, ah, Blake," Jake Trexler said. At their last meeting that was the name Brandon had traveled under, and it came easier to the tongue by now than the original.

"Blake," John B. Parker said, more in the tone of someone labeling an object than of greeting a person. "Nothing. We're not."

"We're not in Bigsbee, that is, so nothing brings us here," Jake Trexler said. "On our way to Cheyenne, stepped out on the platform to stretch our legs while the train stops."

Brandon heard the eruption of a roar from the Grange Hall, which, like the sound of the cyclone, did not die down but increased in volume and menace.

"I think it might be a good idea to get back on the train right now," he said.

Jake Trexler gave him a quick look, turned to John B. Parker, and said, "Up the stairs, Mr. Parker."

"Why?" John B. Parker said. "I don't propose to be pushed here and there on the say-so of some newspaper hack and windmill salesman. John B. Parker didn't get where he is by letting himself—"

The first few men to pelt out of the Grange Hall had reached the platform, and one of them ran up to Brandon, Trexler, and Parker and gasped, "Mr. Parker? Mr. John B. Parker?"

Trexler, eyeing the wave of men leaving the hall and approaching the platform, shook his head and firmly said, "No, he ain't—"

"Why, yes," John B. Parker said. "John B. Parker, and glad of the chance to view your little town before—"

"Glad to meet you, sir," the man said with a grin that bared all his teeth, "happier'n I can say!" He grabbed Parker's right hand and shook it vigorously and clapped him on the left shoulder; two other men from the hall were suddenly behind Parker and between him and Jake Trexler, laying heavy arms on his shoulders and back and easing him down the platform.

Jake Trexler reached inside his coat; Brandon laid a firm hand on his arm. "They've got him now, and they're not going to back down for your gun. All you can do is kill some, and if you do, they'll tear him to pieces, and you and likely me along with him."

"Trexler, damn it, help me!" Parker called. "Let me go, damn you!"

"Who are they, and what do they want with him?" Jake Trexler asked.

"Farmers. They were meeting to see what they could do about freight rates when—"

"The man that sets 'em showed up as if he'd been set out on a tray," Jake Trexler said. "Be calm, Mr. Parker!" he called. "We'll get this set to rights!"

Whether the conductor failed to notice the disturbance on the platform or considered it none of his business, he gave the departure signal, and the train pulled out. "Our bags are on that," Jake Trexler said gloomily.

"Rights is what we're after!" one of the men holding Parker called. "No harm to be done, only justice!"

"If they really mean that, then the old bastard's done for," Jake Trexler muttered.

John B. Parker, comparatively quiet, was being hustled across the road toward the Grange Hall by the dozen or so men surrounding him. "They mean lower rates, I'd say, not overall balancing of the scales of justice, so they'll let him live. You don't care much for him, as I recall."

"Trying to imagine the kind of person that could care for John B. Parker makes my blood run cold," Jake Trexler said. "No surprise he's a lifelong bachelor, as well as a son of a bachelor."

Brandon wondered if his guess about a female of unaccountable tastes exercising a softening influence on Parker was totally wide of the mark. It seemed to him, now that he made a point of recalling, that Parker's hair was a shade or so darker than it had been in Chicago. "Maybe you know some of his weak spots and wouldn't mind telling me," Brandon said.

Jake Trexler shook his head. "I get my pay for taking care of him, and while I do that I can't act against him."

Brandon said patiently, "I need something to use on him, to get him to give in to these farmers enough so they'll let him go. If he's as stubborn as he usually is, they'll both dig in, and something's going to happen to him."

"Well, now," Jake Trexler said, "only way I can do my duty is by stabbing him in the back, huh? At times the job's a pleasure. . . ." He stopped and looked at Brandon. "Did he say something about you and *windmills?*"

Inside the Grange Hall, after a brief but fact-filled conversation with Jake Trexler, Brandon shoved his way through the turbulent crowd to Swicegood's side. John B.

Parker was seated behind the desk normally used by speakers, pressed firmly in place by four farmers.

"This is crazy, you know," Brandon said. "You fellows are as bad as the vigilantes, and you picked the wrong one to mess with."

"You're probably right," Swicegood said morosely. "We got carried away when he turned up, and we can't really keep him, and I don't see as we can turn him loose without getting dropped head-down in the privy. Not that much worse could happen to us than already is, with the freight rates strangling us. If something don't get done about that, some of the boys are going to feel they got nothing to lose by acting foolish."

"I know this Parker some," Brandon said. "And if you'll let me talk to him, I'll try to come up with something that'll do you enough good so it's reasonable to let him go. Wouldn't hurt if you had a couple of hotheads shouting something like 'Garrote him!' now and then."

"With Jere Sublette folks were yelling 'Hang him!' I heard," Swicegood said dubiously. "It's more usual, things like this."

"John B. Parker isn't Sublette," Brandon said. "Garroting's what he worries about, so give him garroting. He won't worry if it's unusual."

John B. Parker called down the wrath of Providence on his captors and compared them unfavorably with the crawling and creeping things of the earth, but without the crackling, energetic venom that Brandon's experience of Parker had led him to expect. Was John B. Parker finally slowing down, aging, or even actually frightened by his situation? None of these seemed likely, but Parker was operating in a different, lower key than Brandon remembered.

After five minutes' talk Brandon was surprised at the response he was getting. Jake Trexler had given him a few chinks in John B. Parker's armor, and he was sticking skewers into them as best he could, with the garroters' chorus at the edge of the crowd and politely expressed regrets that the Grange Hall, being a former barn, harbored spiders and snakes, both of which Parker abhorred. It was not much with which to break down the brutal determination of the Killer Elephant of Wall Street and get on to using the other information Trexler had provided; but in fact he appeared to be making progress.

Brandon saw the anxious faces of Simon Rattner and Chief Hodge at the edge of the crowd and earnestly hoped Hodge would not feel like telegraphing Sheriff Cameron about another insurrection in Bigsbee. Applied this time, Cameron's methods would probably leave the Grange Hall floor an inch deep in blood, some of it Brandon's. He pressed on with his efforts.

"Well, of course you have to make back your investment," Brandon said. "But every farmer that goes out of business means less produce shipped, and your revenues will go down, not up. Your bookkeepers can tell you that. And you keep track of the figures, you can't tell me you don't. Has revenue increased by the amount the rates have gone up, or even at all? You don't have to tell me, for it's none of my business," he said at Parker's sudden glare, "but look it over in your own mind."

Parker thought and emitted a grunt that had the sound of a reluctant assent.

In five more minutes Brandon was writing down a series of instructions that would reduce rates on eastbound shipments of produce during certain months and provide rebates if shipments from one shipper went above certain quantities.

There was one provision to do with loading and offloading that subtly took away about ten percent of the overall benefits the farmers would reap from the agreement, but Brandon left it in unargued. Its presence would provide badly needed balm for the wound he was about to inflict on John B. Parker.

"I'll write out the telegram to my office in Chicago, and

you can send it," Parker said, and the men standing next to the desk cheered.

Brandon slid the pad and pencil he had been using over to Parker, who wrote rapidly. "I'm sending this clear, not in cipher, so you'll know I'm playing straight with you," he said.

"Happy to hear it," Brandon said. When Parker finished writing Brandon picked up the sheet of paper and read. "This after the first sentence, where it says 'COBALT,' what's that? There's no cobalt shipped from here."

"Now that's the one bit of code there is," John B. Parker said. "You see, Blake, anybody can send a telegram and sign it John B. Parker. So I have a code word I put into a wire right after the first sentence that lets the office know it's me sent it and it's okay to act on."

"Ah," Brandon said. "Then it's replaced the old signal, COPPER, has it? Last I heard, COBALT was your sign that the message was to be disregarded. Maybe my information's out of date."

"How the hell do you know about my codes?" John B. Parker said. Parker knew nothing of Trexler's acquaintance with Brandon and, Brandon hoped, was unaware of the fact that Trexler had familiarized himself with more aspects of his employer's business than a strict interpretation of his duties called for.

"There's a reason a newspaperman has an edge in going into business, Mr. Parker," he said smoothly. "We have ways of getting information from all over, and we use them. Before I settled on windmills I considered railroads, and I talked to some fellows, and that's where I got on to your codes; no reason to remember them, really, but you and me having met out in Colorado, they stuck in my mind. And isn't it lucky? You want to cross out COBALT and write in COPPER, or have me do it?"

Parker grimaced, made the change, and handed the paper back to Brandon. As he did so it seemed to Brandon that he glanced at the section on loading and offloading, and his expression softened somewhat. Force of habit had obliged him to give himself a hidden advantage even in an agreement he had not intended to keep, and now he saw the virtues of this prudent course.

Brandon waved the paper in the air and gave a brief summary of what Parker had agreed to, waited till the cheers died down, then made for the door, where Chief Hodge and Simon Rattner still stood.

"If you'll have this sent right out, Chief, and bring the acknowledgment back to the Grangers when it comes, it'll be the best keeping of the peace that's been seen around here for a long time," Brandon said. He turned to Rattner. "You feel like calming down a killer elephant in your office for a while? It's a couple of hours till the next train west, and we'll want to keep Parker happy till he's out of here."

The drinks Simon Rattner produced mellowed John B. Parker faster than Brandon would have expected, and he even managed a rueful appreciation of Brandon's skill in outmaneuvering him. "Any time a COBALT wire comes in to Chicago, the fellows have a good laugh and wonder what some sucker gave me in return," he said. "But COPPER messages, they hop to those and see 'em through. By now they're drawing up the new rate schedules, and they'll have 'em ready for the printers day after tomorrow at the latest. Good whiskey, this, Rattner, even the last drop in the glass. Yes, I will, thanks."

He sipped at the refilled glass and said, "'Course, I could go back to Chicago and cancel those orders out of hand, and even boost the rates till all those farmers that manhandled me went to the poorhouse." He grinned down his long nose, and Brandon had a vision of him trumpeting and trampling helpless, puny humans. "But if I do that—back off from the telegram—word gets around that John B. Parker was buffaloed, and the only way he could get out of it was flat-out lying, and that don't do in business. It ain't like issuing stock and such, where it's expected. In business you got to be able at least to look like you're keeping your word. So I'll let this stand. What the hell, Blake, maybe you're right and I'll make more money this way in the long run."

He heaved a sigh. "I'll tell you fellows, I've had a life any man would envy, knowed and respected as the Killer Elephant of Wall Street, enriched myself by some of the most original means there is, impoverished and crushed any that stood against me and lots more besides, able to eat and drink enough to make me sick any time I want, buy whatever there is to be bought. But I am coming to a time in my life where I see there's something beyond screwing my fellow man in matters of business, no matter how much fun it is. Did you tell me you'd been in St. Louis, Blake?"

"Like I told you in Chicago, not for a long time," Brandon said.

"Rattner?"

"Nice place, St. Louis," Rattner said. "Lots of art, paintings, statues."

"Music, too," John B. Parker said. "Band concerts, orchestras, choruses. St. Louis is a place that has got everything. It's got culture, and it's got the go that makes for good business. And I'm coming around to think things like music can be as important as business—you get to see that if there's someone who knows about it and can make you see it. And there's nothing says a good business head and a feeling for music and such can't go together."

Brandon wondered if whiskey always made John B. Parker maudlin or if it was the combination of the drink with relief at the ending of a tight situation.

The late westbound train pulled out of the station with no arms or heads protruding from the passenger car. Neither John B. Parker nor Jake Trexler was the waving-goodbye kind. Brandon had seen them off, wishing Trexler good luck in his task of keeping Parker's neck unmarked by the garroter's noose.

"Good luck in whatever it is you're up to, Mr. Brandon," Trexler said in a voice that did not carry beyond them. "I didn't know in Colorado, and I don't know now, and I prob'ly shouldn't know, for men who carry extra names in their pockets tend to be doing things detectives are supposed to try to stop. But anyhow, I'll wish you success at it. Maybe one day I'll find out what it is."

Brandon walked through the dusk, the lighted storefronts on Main Street drifting unregarded by him. Nice that Trexler wished him luck, and in spite of the limits imposed by his profession, he would probably sympathize with, even if he could not condone, Brandon's extermination of Gren Kenneally and his gang. Trexler had, after all, seen the dead, bloodied face of Elise Brandon staring up into the night as her body was carried out of the smoldering ruin of Mound Farm.

Brandon's shoulders twitched restlessly. Unease seemed to move through him like a faint electrical current, uncomfortable but just short of pain. To be sure, his progress had so far been almost nonexistent, with no indication that anyone he had encountered might be the Neb or Farmer Dick he sought. Sublette, just possibly, but unlikely; the vigilantes, ruled out. No reason even to look at anyone else. It would take more than Jake Trexler's wishes for success to get things moving. Uncertainty and time wasted were enough to make anyone uneasy, but it seemed to him that there was more than that to it, a sense of anticipation of something unknown mixed with the frustration.

He considered dropping in on Ed Marks and telling him of the day's developments but decided against it. Marks was in a queer mood these days, brooding on something he didn't seem inclined to talk about.

Down the street he saw the red and gold sign Carl Swanson had made for Wen Hing, with light gilding the roadway in front of it; it had become almost full dark while he walked.

The patch of light in front of the laundry was broken by an emerging customer, and Brandon stopped in midstep.

Deathwind

The wiry figure with its broad-brimmed hat and leather clothing was unmistakable, and its presence where it was, profoundly astonishing. That Ned Norland should have found his way to Bigsbee, Nebraska, was not in itself particularly remarkable; Norland had been almost everyplace there was in the West. But Ned Norland and a laundry . . . that juxtaposition went beyond the astonishing to the bizarre. Nothing in his experience of Ned Norland had suggested that he was even aware of the concept of clean clothes.

22

The only place in Bigsbee where Ned Norland would have felt truly at home was now deserted, partly window-less, chewed up by gunfire, and bloodstained in places. Brandon's room in the hotel made an acceptable substitute, as it had two chairs to sit in, light to see by, and a table to support the bottle of whiskey Brandon bought at the bar downstairs.

"You didn't know I was here, so you didn't come to see me," Brandon said. "What brings you to Bigsbee?"

Ned Norland gulped at his drink and peered at him from under eyebrows like twists of long-dried Spanish moss. "Wrong and wrong. This child knowed you was here and wouldn't no way have set foot amidst the toilers of the earth that is spreadin' the farm mange acrost what useter be God's country till He leased it out to a lot of plow jockeys except he had a reason for seekin' you out."

The uneasiness and tension that had washed through him in the street just before he saw Norland were intense now, and he felt an almost alarmed expectancy. "Then how did you know I was here?"

Norland tossed a string-tied bundle on the table. "I was told what I needed to know to git these to you."

Brandon untied the string and opened the wrapping. He found himself looking at Jess Marvell's meticulous handwriting, single lines and short paragraphs, each headed by a date: one of her reports of whatever information crossed her or Rush Dailey's path that could bear on the mission Brandon had so vaguely outlined for her.

Brandon looked up at Norland. "Who told . . ."

"Miss Jess, natcherly," said Ned Norland, who had never, so far as Brandon had known up to this minute, laid eyes on Jess Marvell. "She'd sent these so as they'd get to wherever you was at, but then she and I confabulated some, and it seemed best I come and deliver 'em to you personal."

Brandon looked at Ned Norland. The old mountain man seemed to flicker, and it was not the effect of the steady flame topping the wick of the coal-oil lantern or of the mouthful or so of whiskey he had taken. He felt a powerful shiver wrench him, as if he had been struck with the ague.

Norland had not brought the reports out here; Jess Marvell had "sent them so as they'd get to wherever" Brandon was, and Norland had picked them up for the final delivery. At Wen Hing's. Wen Hing certainly meant a connection to the tong lord Tsai Wang in San Francisco, who had more than once demonstrated his knowledge of Brandon's whereabouts, under whatever alias he might be traveling. So Jess Marvell had resorted to forwarding this set of reports through Tsai Wang—and if she knew about Tsai Wang, she knew at least ten times as much about Cole Brandon and his chosen mission than he had ever dreamed or wanted.

He felt another wrenching chill, as if he were being transformed into something else, like the werewolves Marija Svarog had told him of down in Texas, humans who changed into animals. His picture of himself as a lone hunter, casting about for an elusive scent and following it until he made the kill, rearranged itself painfully in his mind, turning into a giant, shadowy board with obscure divisions on which he and the

Kenneally gang made seemingly random jumps while
other pieces or perhaps players moved in the mist-
shadowed corners of the board, and it was suddenly hard
to know what the goal of the game was or how victory or
defeat could be determined.

"Don't need to go through all of 'em," Ned Norland
said. "Just one thing in there that consarns you, word
from a couple places that Gren Kenneally's goin' t' be in
Philadelphy this summer, along with the world an' his
wife. Gren ain't inter'sted in improvin' his mind by
inspectin' the cultivations and manufacturosities of the
civilized world and Californy, my bet bein' that with so
many visitors expositioning, nobody won't hardly take
notice of a bunch of fellers gettin' together and finally
sharin' out the proceeds from that train robbery."

As far as Brandon and Ned Norland had been able to
learn at the time, Gren Kenneally had disappeared with
most of the train loot, leaving the others with the
promise of a reunion for the share-out when possible, a
hope that seemed to have faded for many of them.

Brandon shook his head to try to clear it. "Kenneally's
mentioned in the report?" Ned Norland nodded. A main
reason for the vagueness of the commission Brandon had
given Jess Marvell and Rush Dailey was that taking an
interest in Kenneally affairs could be extremely dangerous; now it appeared that Jess Marvell had found her way
past that barrier and disregarded it.

He looked at Ned Norland and wondered if his idea of
the old mountain man had any basis in reality, if he knew
anybody as accurately as he thought he did. Maybe
Simon Rattner was a dedicated embezzler, maybe
Swicegood ran his farm to disguise the tunnel he was
digging to admit the forces of the emperor of Brazil to
conquer the United States; neither of those would be any
more improbable than the revision of his picture of Jess
Marvell that was being forced on him.

"And there's a rumor that Gren will be there?" Brandon said.

"More than a rumor," Ned Norland said. "I was there, seein' to it that the knee bones connected to the thigh bones and the thigh bones connected to the hip bones and such, for the perfessers' lizard display, and I seen him in the crowds as is wanderin' through, even before the Exposition opens."

So far as Brandon knew, Ned Norland had never seen Gren Kenneally, but it seemed silly now to raise that point; if Norland said he had seen Gren, he had, and why wonder about it?

"Could have follered him and corpsed him and made an end to it all," Ned Norland said. "But he weren't mine to kill. Yours, Brandon, and no one's else."

Brandon looked absently at the papers, turning them over until the name Kenneally appeared, the first time he had seen it in Jess Marvell's handwriting. He started to read it, but the letters swam as his eyes slipped out of focus. What it meant, taken with Ned Norland's sighting of Gren Kenneally, was that Kenneally and most of the rest of the survivors of his gang would be in one place at one time. Four or five of them against one; not good odds, but to die in the middle of shortening them was one way he had always known this could end.

And it was time for it to end, he knew now. The lives he had led fragments of, the work he had done, though put on only to further his vengeance, had enlarged Cole Brandon rather than replacing him. He had learned things, done things, seen things that Cole Brandon, Esq., partner in Lunsford Ahrens & Brandon, never would have. The result was a new man who had not existed before, and that man, if he lived, would have a life the old Cole Brandon could not have imagined.

Could Krista be part of that life? So much of what he had experienced since leaving St. Louis suggested that he had become someone who could not mesh with her; yet the completion of his mission might return him more closely to his former self than he now thought likely. If, that is, she were still available, though, he recalled, her forthrightness and uncanny business ability had always made her less than sought-after among St. Louis's conventional middle-class beaux.

Or Jess Marvell . . . No sensible way to think of either of them until it was done. All the more reason for getting it done soon. Brandon realized that he was as impatient to live again, if he were to live, as to achieve his deadly goal.

And of course there was something else, something he had not wanted to think that closely about, but it was there and could not be put off any longer.

He looked up to ask Ned Norland's counsel, but the place opposite him was marked only by an empty glass. Norland had vanished so silently that only the glass and the bundle of reports proved that he had been there. Brandon wondered if he would see Ned Norland again and decided that, if he had to, he would; one of those ambiguous, shadowed figures in the corners of the board would see to it.

But this he would have to work out on his own. He looked closely at Jess Marvell's report and turned over in his mind some conversations in the last few days. A man owed some money in Philadelphia, a man with an aversion to trains because they meant trouble, a man who had come here to farm but had to find another business, a man wondering about why he had done what he had done . . .

Ed Marks.

Brandon knew that as a defense attorney he would have no trouble refuting any connection between Ed Marks and the Mound Farm killings, or any crime whatever. In fact, a defense attorney would have no function; there wasn't a tenth of the evidence needed for an indictment. But he was utterly sure, with a certainty born of days of unconscious weighing and collating of what Ed Marks had said, that Marks was the "Farmer Dick" he had come to Nebraska to find and kill.

And he was also the man who had saved Brandon's life on the stairs at the Seagull.

Brandon walked through the night streets of Bigsbee, slowly and deliberately. What he would decide he did not know, but he would decide it by the time he got to the livery stable. He had the .38 in his pocket in case the decision went one way.

Back in New Mexico Brandon had had Peter Kenneally, Gren's brother and companion at Mound Farm, in his sights, and let him go. Shooting him would have broken the silence of an ambush and ruined the mission of the unofficial law enforcement group he had helped train, and imperiled the lives of men who trusted him. Peter Kenneally had found a death a good deal more painful than Brandon would have dealt him, but Brandon had no way of knowing that at the time. Brandon had thought that nothing loomed larger in his life than retribution but found that an undertaken obligation did.

And was there an obligation here? When Ed Marks shot Walter Kitson it was an almost automatic action, not a deliberate saving of Brandon's—of Calvin Blake's—life. Yet without it Brandon and Blake and any future identities they might yet spin out would not exist.

Seems as if he's broken with Gren, Brandon thought. Doesn't want to go to Philadelphia to collect the money he's owed, "not worth it," which you can take to mean he's sickened by what he did. He was nearing the sign in front of the livery stable when he found he had decided. I let Peter go because of what I owed the other men there. I'm letting Marks live because of what I owe myself.

But there's one thing left to do. He'll have to know who I am and that I know who he is. If he can know that and let go of it, then so can I.

Brandon quickened his steps toward the stable, feeling the weight of the pistol in his pocket. He stepped inside, then stopped as he saw the slight figure of Ed Marks's helper, Sam, filling a canvas feed bucket.

"Help you?" Sam said.

"Looking to talk to Ed," Brandon said.

"Need a horse or rig, I can fit you out," Sam said. "Ed left me in charge."

"For how long?" Brandon asked.

Sam shrugged. "Didn't say. Went off yesterday, told me to run the business for a few days. Looking to find out about getting into a new line of work, he tolt me. You want a horse?"

"No," Brandon said. "I think I'll be taking the train."

23

As it turned out, Brandon did not leave Bigsbee by train.

"The river started acting crazy after the storm that come with the twister," the ticket clerk said when Brandon went to the station to purchase a place on the late-afternoon eastbound train, "and yesterday it took out one of the bridges between here and Platteville. When the eastbound train comes she'll stop here, and we'll load any passengers into a buggy or a cart or whatever it needs to hold 'em. You're welcome to a seat on that, and the railroad won't charge fare but from Platteville east."

Brandon decided he would rather not either wait for the train or take his chances on being dumped in with an indeterminate number of eastbound passengers in any vehicle that would accommodate them, and he returned to Ed Marks's stable, finding Sam still on duty.

"You can leave it at Jim Draper's place in Platteville," Sam said as he saddled the horse Brandon had hired. "I think it was Jim's to start with, but it's gone back and forth a bunch of times. Time it is now, be nightfall 'fore you get there, but the track's good, and the horse knows the way."

Brandon left Bigsbee with no more sense of regret than he had any of the half dozen or so places he had lived in during his mission. The only thing left undone was his confrontation with Ed Marks, but if that had not happened, it was probably not meant to happen.

He did not turn aside at the Kitson farm, now the Kitson-Swanson farm. Goodbyes seemed unneeded; all they did was announce that you were going, which, once you were no longer around, was self-evident.

The scattered flimsy-looking windmills that broke the line of the level plain or gentle hills prompted a feeling of proprietary pride in him, which he quickly suppressed. There's no sense getting puffed up over what's only part of a disguise, he thought, stage business that goes with the role. But I *was* a pretty good salesman, and someday I'll get that thousand back from Nonpareil.

He followed the same road he had with Simon Rattner, past the farms and to within sight of the hill from which they had been fired on.

His mind drifted to Rattner, the banker and art lover, then to John B. Parker, brutal businessman and, recently, patron of music and admirer of St. Louis . . . and behaving in many ways like a man mellowed by a developing attachment to a woman—a younger woman, judging by the steady reclaiming of Parker's hair by the forces of blackness. . . .

After a while Brandon became aware that his mind was a blank, and that its state was caused by the need to keep two sets of facts completely apart.

It had taken him a while yesterday to allow himself to admit what he had come to know about Ed Marks. And now there was something else making every effort to make itself known to him that he seemed not to want to know.

Something to do with John B. Parker, with St. Louis, with music, with music in St. Louis, with Brandon and Elise at concerts with Krista . . .

The horse stopped in protest as Brandon's heels dug into it. Last night he had felt his world turned upside down when he discovered new faces on Ned Norland and Jess Marvell; now he felt as if his very self had been turned inside out, like a rabbit being skinned.

Krista's statement of a possible new course . . . Parker's interest in St. Louis, in music . . . Krista's strength and business acumen, appealing only to a man who valued such things . . . her sometimes shockingly honest realism about what was and was not possible . . . As with Ed Marks, no proof that would get near enough a court to be laughed out of it, but, once thought of, clearly and dreadfully the truth.

It was as near a certainty as the darkness that would follow the just-completed sunset that Elise Ostermann Brandon's sister was on the point of an alliance with a connection, admittedly distant, of the man who had brought about Elise's murder.

Brandon rode on through the gathering dusk, sometimes thinking of windmills, once coming up with a picture of himself with an oversized lance, attacking them under the impression that they were giants, like poor crazy old Don Quixote. Sometimes thinking of the cave he had wandered through for what seemed like days in Arizona, sometimes thinking of Jess Marvell, and succeeding pretty well in not thinking very much at all about Krista Ostermann and John B. Parker.

It was full night, with a pale sliver of moon picking out shapes of trees and hills as he passed, and he was drowsing, letting the horse carry him along, staying conscious enough to keep his seat. Tsai Wang in San Francisco was saying something nasty about Gren Kenneally when Brandon felt something cold jammed against his head just behind the left ear.

"Keep awful still, mister," a voice next to him grated. Brandon felt the bulk of a horse's flank against his leg and realized that the other rider had with silent skill matched pace with his horse and moved next to him while he nodded.

The metal was withdrawn from his head, and the voice in the darkness said, "The gun's still on you, and I can see well enough to drill you whereat I want to, so slide off the horse and lie flat." The voice was muffled, and Brandon suspected a mask like those the vigilantes had worn.

A reach for the .38 in his trousers pocket would clearly occasion the response the holdup man had threatened, and Brandon dismounted and lay facedown on the trail.

Footsteps approached and stopped, the gun muzzle again nestled against his head, and a hand patted his jacket and trousers pockets and pulled out his wallet and the pistol. "Next we sees what's in the saddlebags," the bandit said, "and then—"

Brandon, his right arm shadowed by an overhanging tree, snaked his hand into his vest and pulled out the single-shot .30-caliber pistol, brought up his arm just as the bandit was turning away from the horse and lifting his weapon to bear on Brandon, fired, and leapt to one side. If the shot missed, dodging was the only defense left.

The holdup man's head snapped back, then forward. He stood still for an instant, his gun hand hanging down, then relaxing its grip, and then his right leg buckled, and he toppled sideways to the ground.

Brandon picked himself up from the ground, brushing at the knees of his trousers, one of which had not survived the impact with a sharp rock. The bandit lay still, a dark shape in the pale moonlight. Brandon found a match in his pocket, struck it on a stone, and knelt.

A black handkerchief covered the face. Brandon lifted it and saw Ed Marks staring sightlessly at him.

Brandon sighed and stood up. Not a good new line of business for him to take up, he thought; less successful at it than at the last one. Seems as if it doesn't matter what I think about this, what I decide to do. If I'm meant to kill them, I kill them.

And now there's Gren and the rest, in Philadelphia now, or will be. And me on my way there, to fill out the picture. I guess whatever's supposed to happen there will happen, too. Nice if I get the chance to look back on it and figure it out.

Brandon dragged Marks's body off the trail into the brush and slapped his riderless horse, sending it trotting back toward Bigsbee with an indignant whinny.

He retrieved his .38 from where Marks had dropped it and the .30 from where he had flung it after firing it, stowed them in trousers and vest, and remounted. For a moment it struck him as odd that he was riding a horse still the legal property of the man he had just killed.

With the thought that there wasn't much out here that wasn't odd, Brandon rode ahead into the dark.